I0750061

ISBN 978-0-692-88336-5

Cover Design by Conor Reed

Abraham

A Fiction Installment in

You Are Abraham

A Multimedia Story by

Daniel Backer

www.YouAreAbraham.com

Part 1

Tom Downey's

Chapter 1

Your body flinched at the sensation of falling when you realized you didn't have the slightest recollection of driving to Los Angeles. Come to think of it, you couldn't remember how you'd cracked the back of your head. You touched your fingers to the wettest part of the gauze, and as your fingers grazed the crack, a searing pain flashed through your skull, and your field of view rippled and puckered with pulsing waves of pain.

You swerved on the road and cried out. A string of drool dripped from your gaping mouth. The pain in your head radiated down your spine, and tears rolled down your cheeks. A pull on your insides threatened to drain you through the bottom of your car seat when a booming horn from an 18-wheeler behind you brought you back to your senses.

You managed to drive to an exit, and you ascended the first hill in sight to recoup in the cover of the trees. You pulled over and rested your aching head on the steering wheel, whimpering. An electronic voice told you, "You have arrived at your destination." You squinted at the GPS navigation on your dashboard. It read "6835 Pacific View Dr." To your left, hedges towered twenty feet into the air, and there was a steel-gated entrance with a call button under a security camera that protruded from the wall and stared out next to a number plate that, sure enough, read "6835."

You got out of the car and hobbled toward the call button. You were wearing dark sunglasses, a dirty white t-shirt, and gray sweatpants. You looked normal except for the gauze bandage around your head. The slack-jawed, blank look on your face didn't help either. There was an enormous brown bloodstain on the back of your shirt from the bloody crack on the back of your head.

You pushed the call button by the gate. The protruding security camera snaked up to look you in the eye, and a disjointed, mechanical voice asked through the speaker, "Greetings. What is your business with Mr. Downey?"

"Downey?" you asked.

"Yes," the mechanical voice answered. "What is your business with Mr. Downey?"

"I'm not sure, actually. What's Mr. Downey's first name?"

"Tom."

Tom Downey? That didn't ring any bells.

The mechanical voice repeated, "What is your business with Mr. Downey?" Though the voice's inflection didn't change, the repetition seemed to communicate some mechanical impatience.

"I don't know," you stammered. "I just kind of rolled up… My GPS told me to come here… I'm Abraham."

"Ha," the voice laughed in a single staccato note. "Why didn't you say so? Mr. Downey has invited you to stay with him."

"Cool… why?"

"Mr. Downey does not disclose patient detail to me."

"What, is he a doctor?"

The voice gave the same lifeless *Ha*. "That is a good one. Mr. Downey is a monk."

"Okay… And, who are you?"

"I am a general intelligence simulator that Mr. Downey built. I have no name."

"Well, nice to meet you anyway."

"Certainly. Right this way, Abraham."

The gate opened silently, and a long path up what seemed like a mountain lay before you. White lotus flowers filled the air with the scent of damp blossoming, and rows of pink cedars crowded among the squirming roots of ficus trees so overgrown that their thick foliage blocked out the sky. As you looked up, a gust of wind parted the branches, and little traces of light appeared on the path.

What might have been a temple at the top of the mountain turned out to be a mansion. It looked like a Rubik's cube had been disassembled and dropped from the sky, and the individual pieces had crashed into the hills. Each cube of the house was a different color: a red cube, a blue cube, a green cube, and one cube that was white, but with various moving, colorful lights projected on it.

You heard laughter coming from the back yard, so you circled around on a stone footpath that was lined with Buddha statues, gongs, and Asian symbols painted on rocks. In the backyard, there were tall cedar trees planted along the edges of a 30-foot-high protective wall.

You found Tom sitting in a hot tub with virtual reality goggles strapped to his face, and he was cackling about whatever he was experiencing inside of them. He was heavy and almost completely bald on top. He had gray hair on the sides of his head and on his chest. His saffron robes lay in a heap on the ground next to the hot tub.

After shuffling awkwardly for a moment, you gently tapped him on the shoulder, and he took off his VR goggles, startled. It took a moment for his eyes to adjust.

"Who goes there?"

"Me… Abraham."

"Of course! I've been expecting you. Welcome to the next chapter in your life." Tom stood to climb out of the hot tub, and you saw that he was completely naked.

You looked away, pretending to marvel at his garden while he dried off and put his saffron robes back on. He rolled his head back and forth, cracking his neck. He balanced on one foot, and for a moment he hummed what sounded like an ancient mantra. Handing you the virtual reality goggles, he said, "Take 'em for a spin."

You put them on, plugged in the earbuds, but your vision was so blurry that you could barely tell that you were face-to-face with a naked woman who was giving you a virtual lap dance. You could tell that that was what it was only by hearing her promising to do whatever you wanted. You peeked back into the real world, a little embarrassed.

"Pretty cool, huh?" Tom said, smiling.

"Right on," you said, handing the goggles back to Tom. You let go before he had them, and they fell into the hot tub. You and Tom watched them sink slowly.

Tom finally said, "That's alright. I have more..."

"Isn't that against the rules, anyway?"

"What rules?"

"Monk rules?"

Tom laughed. "So, I'm not allowed to jack off every once in a while?"

"I don't know," you said, eyeing the bubbles in the hot tub suspiciously.

"I embrace the Buddhist Middle Way. As long as I avoid extremes, I can pretty much do whatever I want," Tom said, with a menacing smile.

You backed away from him, panicking and whimpering oddly at his sudden shift.

"Abraham. Relax, dude. I was joking." He reached a hand out toward you, and you jerked away in fear.

Tom showed you his hands to show that he meant no harm. He squinted at you and pointed to his mouth, "...you've got a little..." You brought your hand to your chin. You'd been drooling.

"Sorry."

"That bump on your head was more serious than I thought."

You looked to Tom helplessly, asking, "Do you think I should go to a hospital?"

"You already did," he said, pointing to your

hospital bracelet. You had not noticed it before now. "How much do you remember?"

You squinted your eyes, straining to remember, but there were no epiphanies. You lost balance from trying to think so hard and stumbled forward. Tom caught you just before you hit the ground.

"It's okay. I've got you." He stood you back on your feet. "I will take care of you here."

You became teary and desperate. "Do you really think you can help me?"

Tom was quiet for a moment. He turned away, saying, "The junior varsity quarterback for my high school got hit with a devastating tackle in the final game of his senior year. Even though it ended his football career, it awakened poetry in his brain, and he's a best-selling writer now. But, Charles Whitman, the Texas Town Shooter, never shot anybody until a tumor started pressing against certain parts of his brain. Material changes like that can go either way."

"So?"

"So, I'm going to do everything in my power to coax you toward the former."

"And, what if I'm the latter?"

"It's more of a spectrum, but frankly, I don't think you'll turn out to be the violent type. Judging by the drooling situation, we're going to spend most of our time trying to get you to behave like a human. No offense.. We can take this crack on your head as an opportunity to restart. Reprogram, if you will."

"I just want to get back to normal."

"Normal? When I'm through with you, you will be transformed. You're about to embark on an amazing journey. You're going to grow and change into the best version of yourself and have a bona fide story to tell afterward."

"I don't know. My crack is pretty sensitive. And, I've been seeing some weird—"

Tom excitedly interrupted, "What have you seen?"

Tom's outline became very blurry, and the sky seemed to melt, descend, and wrap around him.

"Nothing crazy, just foggy vision," you replied. Tom seemed disappointed. "Also… How did I get here? And, who are you?"

"I'm a friend of your father's."

You nodded as though that clarified matters, "How's he doing?"

Tom stared at you. After a moment, he said, "Abraham, I hope you're not offended, but I would like to run a test on you in order to… gauge the severity of your situation."

He waited for your reply until you shrugged.

He nodded politely before disappearing inside his house, leaving you to stand alone in his backyard, staring at nothing in particular, blank. The wind whistled softly.

Tom emerged, wheeling a cart with an old TV on it, and a long orange extension cord trailing from it. He parked it next to you, and turned it on. A cartoon alien was flying around a spacecraft, chasing an astronaut with typical cartoonish antics that defied physics. Tom had to turn you toward the TV, and adjust your head so that he was sure you were watching.

You gazed at the screen, puzzled. The cartoon alien and astronaut appeared to you as cloudy shapes moving around the screen. Bored, you looked away to Tom's house and stared there instead.

Tom frowned. "Abraham, your journey and transformation are going to take a lot of work, and I need to make sure that you are 100% committed to the task at hand."

"That's alright. It was nice to meet you, Tom."

You turned and started walking toward the gate.

Tom said, "I can assure you that you will never return to normal if you don't accept this journey."

You turned on your heel, and inelegantly ran back to Tom. You tripped and fell and grabbed at his saffron robes.

You blubbered, "I'm willing to do whatever it takes."

Tom looked away, embarrassed for you.

"First things first. Don't be desperate. It's off-putting. Let's hit a bar. I haven't gotten laid in a long time."

Chapter 2

The bar was a dive on Sunset in Echo Park called the Dark Room. There were red bulbous shades around the hanging light bulbs, giving everything a red glow. The walls were covered in Polaroid photos, and you could pay a dollar to take a picture and post it on the wall with a thumbtack. It bothered you that they decided to go with Polaroid photos, which did not require a darkroom to be developed.

The loud club music they had blaring made it difficult to hear Tom. When you complained about the volume, he replied blankly, "It's ladies night. They can't turn down the music on ladies night." Two women dressed in all black sat down next to Tom, and he spun on his bar stool. You watched him hit on them, and when they were unreceptive to his advances, he turned to the bartender and said something while holding up two fingers. The women walked away before the drinks arrived. Tom spun back toward you, and you caught the end of his saying, "… hard to get. Thirsty?"

The two of you pounded beers for an hour or so. Tom shouted over the music about this and that. You were silent. He was full of recommendations. "This place in Santa Monica called Horny's has the best oysters on the half shell on this planet. Period. And, they only serve aphrodisiacs, so finding someone there who wants to bang is a piece of cake.

"And, there's a shoe boutique that I've been

hanging at on Fairfax called Dope-amine. It's all right. But, the chicks who work there are hot, so I've been buying a lot of shoes. Remember these?" Tom lifted the hem of his saffron robe, revealing his shoes, which had a single wheel in each heel that you could glide on. "I've had a few close calls walking down the stairs... But, if you're looking for a tapas place, you have to try Bee Jay's."

"I don't know if I'd be comfortable at a strip club."

"T-A-P-A-S. It's shit served on little plates. And, they have the biggest ones in town. The waitresses there are so-so. But, the tapas are really what I go for. If you want a strip club though, pretty much any place on Hollywood Boulevard will do you just fine. Oh! They have a float center in Westwood. Very therapeutic. Very healing."

"Float tank?"

"It's a tank of body-temperature water with Epsom salts dissolved in it, and you float in the dark, deprived of sensory input."

"For how long?"

"Usually for a few hours."

"Why would I want to do that?"

"You'll have to see for yourself. You go in to surrender to the darkness, and it elevates your awareness and gets in touch with the source of consciousness. It's like hot-wiring the meditation process. Have you been meditating like I taught you?"

"Oh, every now and again," you lied. You had no memory of Tom's teaching you to meditate.

"You should really do it every day. It's the best

way to get over your predicament. What mantra have you been using?"

"Uh…"

"*Ohm*? You'd do better with *sat, nam. Sat* on the exhale, *nam* on the inhale."

"What does that mean?"

"You're not supposed to know. If you focus on these ancient words that have no meaning to you, the turbulence of the mind will settle, and you'll be immersed in…"

Tom's voice was drowned out by the music. You asked him to repeat, but he'd already started saying, "Floating will change the game for you. I hate what the salt water does to my hair, so I had to buy this fancy shampoo. They don't sell it in most stores, but there's a salon in Brentwood that sells it." You thought that it was odd that Tom cared about his hair. There was so little of it. "There's a stylist there named Samantha that I've had my eye on, so I might need to pick up some shampoo tomorrow."

What you shouted back at him was mostly, "Cool… I'll have to check it out sometime… Nice," etc. You couldn't tell if he could hear you over the music; and if he could, you weren't sure that he was listening. Tom was more of a talker.

"So, how many girls have you slept with since you've been out here?" he asked.

"I just got here at like two o'clock."

"Yea, but it's five now."

"Touché."

"So, zero?"

"Yea. But, after one day, that's not bad."

"It's not good either."

You looked at the sea of people laughing, dancing, and gesticulating animatedly, and among them were a few gorgeous women.

"Abraham, go talk to her." Tom subtly pointed at a girl who was looking at you coyly and idly playing with her hair. "She's giving you the signs."

"That could mean anything."

"Abraham. You get the fuck over there, and talk to that girl."

As you shifted in your seat, you realized that the beers had affected you more strongly than you had expected. It looked like Tom was rocking back and forth, but then it became clear that the entire bar was shifting in your perception, and before you could stop yourself, you were falling off the bar stool onto the cold tile of the floor.

You woke up in a sleeping bag on the floor next to a king-sized bed in a brilliantly white room. As your eyes adjusted to the morning light, you waited for your brain to wake up all the way to make sense of where you were. Still nothing. You were certain you had never been there before. You rose from the sleeping bag and saw that you were in a loft that overlooked a living room that had a big-screen TV in front of red and orange blobs that may or may not have been furniture and a bookshelf built into the wall.

There was a ladder that went from the loft to the living room, and you wondered how you had climbed up in your drunkenness. Had you been carried? Had you drunkenly broken into someone's house? The last thing you remembered was seeing Tom's hand reaching for you as you fell backwards off the barstool. It must have been more of a crumpling to the floor than a deadweight fall because you were not particularly sore or in pain anywhere. Except for your hangover that had been slowly intensifying. And, except for the wound that still bled slowly under the gauze on the back of your head. But, that had already been there.

You hoped that no one was home, so you could slip out the front door, and get off the property of wherever you were. You made your way down the ladder and out the back door next to the bookshelves, and you finally saw the hot tub and tall cedars in the back yard.

It came as a huge relief that you were at Tom's. You wouldn't have to worry about explaining how you'd trespassed and conked out in some stranger's house. But, what had happened last night? Maybe the beers had made you do something terrible. A distinct shame descended over you. It was hard enough to account for your behavior after you had bumped your head. Now it seemed like there had been a you parading around and doing god knows what without your permission.

Back inside, you saw that your shoes had been neatly placed next to one of the orange pieces of modern furniture or whatever it was supposed to be. The thought of Tom's taking your shoes off gave you the creeps. You sat on the orange blob in front of the TV, and after failing to find a comfortable position, you decided it was not furniture after all.

Your phone dinged in your pocket, and a

notification from Tom told you that he had booked you an appointment at the Westwood Float Center at four o'clock. It took you a moment to decipher the counter-clockwise-moving hands on a novelty, analogue clock that Tom had in the living room. It was only eleven. You decided to watch some TV.

You found a basket that was full of remote controls, and you tried a few, and finally you found one that turned the TV on, and you clicked as many combinations of buttons as you could think of, but all of them yielded various menu screens for adjusting the brightness of the screen or input modes for external devices.

You gave up and browsed the shelves that were in the walls of the living room. Most of Tom's books were in classical Greek and what appeared to be Sanskrit.

You left the living room, and entered another living room. This one was full of Victorian furniture and what looked like a soundproof recording booth with a microphone in it. There was an old-school mixing board and a few boxes and pads that had all sorts of knobs and buttons on them, stacked in a corner next to a few expensive-looking guitars and a drum set. Tom was a musician and a monk and a VR enthusiast? Where did he find the time?

You left the second living room and entered what turned out to be a bowling alley that was ancient Greece-themed, with regal pillars separating the lanes and a fully stocked bar and a clear glass urn full of marijuana on the counter. There were various colorful pipes in front of the urn on a cloth that had the words "just one more bowl" and a smoking bowling ball cross-stitched on it.

At the end of the room, there were saloon-style swinging doors that seemed out of place with the otherwise ancient-Grecian bowling alley. The doors led into a massive showroom full of taxidermied animals mounted on the walls. Tom had the heads of hippos, alligators, lions, and even sheep. One corner of the room had a small log cabin in it, with one of the walls removed. Inside the cabin was a fireplace, various pipes, and two zebra rugs on the floor.

You knew very little about Tom's philosophy or religion if any, but having a bunch of dead animals as decorations seemed incongruent with any spiritual practice. You hoped you would remember to ask him about it later, but even moments after making the mental note, you had forgotten what you were supposed to be remembering.

A door in the back of the small log cabin led you into a hallway that had pictures of all of the presidents except for the last picture, which was of Tom himself. There was a bonsai tree in front of his picture on an end table pressed against the wall. You reached to touch it, but the voice of the nameless general intelligence simulator said authoritatively, "Don't touch that."

You recoiled, and eyed the room with a new suspicion. Knowing you were being watched, you trying to play it cool. You asked, "How's it going?"

"I'm good. I hope you are doing well too."

You nodded, satisfied.

Past the picture of Tom, there was a hallway of

doors that were all different—ones you'd need to crawl through to enter, double doors with elaborate lion door knockers and hand-carved wooden handles, a door that when you touched your hand to it was revealed to be just a painted outline of a door on the wall, a standard wooden door that was uncharacteristic but added to the variety with its plainness, and an enormous steel door like a bank vault. It had bolted plates around the edge of the doorframe and a huge dial on the front.

You felt a cold pang in the crack in the back of your head. This last door scared you for some reason. Why the enormous lock? You were certain that some evil lurked behind this door. You rushed away from the large steel door, through the hallway of presidential pictures, into the tiny log cabin and the taxidermy showroom, past the swinging saloon-style doors, through the ancient Grecian bowling alley, through the second living room with the recording booth, and finally into the room which you'd woken up in that morning. Your heart was pounding in your chest.

But, then you started laughing when you realized that you'd gotten worked up over a door. The dead animals should have been much more frightening. You caught your breath and exited a swinging door in the living room and found yourself in the kitchen. There was an enormous pig tied to the handle on the stove. It grunted at your entrance. Though you were alarmed at first, he seemed to be peaceful enough.

You stomped toward a door that you thought would take you outside, but it was a closet full of saffron robes. You tried another door that revealed a shrine with a statue of Buddha playing the electric guitar. You finally opened a door that led to the back yard. You found Tom's sunglasses next to the hot tub. You put them on.

Chapter 3

By the time you got to your car and started driving, you were already picturing the landscape to be a vibrant affirmation of life—palm trees with explosions of lush fronds like celebratory fireworks on top of their trunks; thick coral trees holding their arms up as if to say *Ta-da*; fuzzy puffs of flowers that would bob like fishing lures in the sweet-smelling breeze; and glistening oranges, lemons, and limes ornamenting the trees behind white picket fences. The sun high above would give everything a singular glow; and at night, light would seem to emanate from the city itself.

But, the sun was somewhere else today.

You felt a wet drop on the back of your neck. Rain? That would ruin your entire grand entrance. Oh, never mind. It was blood. You must have bled through the gauze. There would probably be a pharmacy around before too long, where you could restock on antiseptic and bandages.

Black exhaust fumes and rancid trash smell from the garbage truck in front of you slid over your windshield and into your face. You got a hot inhale, and you gagged. The convertible top would have to go up. This would have to be as windblown as your hair got today.

And, it was so overcast that wearing Tom's sunglasses was at best unnecessary and at worst dangerous. It wouldn't hurt to take off the shades, if only to see the road better.

You parked on the street at a plaza in Westwood. The antique bulbous streetlights were ornately decorated with garlands and hanging baskets of flowers, and people on the sidewalks huddled in their puffy coats with fur around the hoods, and skittered out of storefronts to their cars. Your teeth were chattering by the time you found the float center's storefront.

You entered, and a grunge guy with straight hair past his ears and faded jeans greeted you and signed you in. There was a sense of deep peace about him, an unpretentious calmness.

"So, have you ever floated before?"

"First time."

"I'm very excited for you." Someone else might have shown their excitement by smiling and nodding. The way this guy showed his excitement was by looking you in the eye and telling you sincerely that he was excited

"Wear these," he said, handing you a pair of earplugs. "You don't want any salt to get in your ears because it can harden. Afterward, shower and fill your ear with water…"

He tilted his head to the side to demonstrate, and even though you could tell he'd done it many times, he was gently attentive, at once perfunctory and engaged.

"… And, tilt it out…" He tilted his head the other way to show how to drain the water out, and as he did you could almost feel water draining out of your own ear. "Don't wave your hand in front of your face, because you'll drip salt water into your eyes. There's a hand towel on the inside door handle for when you inevitably wave your hand in front of your face."

"Should I be worried about my crack situation in the water?" You pointed at the back of your head.

"Hmm," the grunge guy walked behind you to get a better look. "It's definitely a health concern. But, you can just go in."

"Really?"

"I won't tell anyone. And, you can lock the door. No one can enter from the outside."

"But, is it bad for me? For the crack?"

"The tank heals all things."

He looked at you intently, and you blinked at him, unconvinced.

The grunge guy led you to your float tank and left promptly without saying goodbye. There was a shower on one wall and a metal door on another. That must be the tank. You turned on the shower and washed your whole body, especially careful when washing around your gauze bandage.

You opened the metal door of the tank, and there was less water than you had expected there to be. You frowned. The light that spilled in from the outside showed you little pieces of something floating in the water. The rubber lining of the tank bubbled up in various places, probably from the humidity.

You stepped down into the pool, and the water was colder than you'd have liked. You sat down, and with that little tickle you used to get when you'd hide in hide-and-seek, you shut the heavy door behind you, and you were immersed in darkness.

It was actually almost darkness, but the outdoor light had apparently stained your eyes, like when you look at a light bulb or the sun too long, and though the door was closed, you could still imagine where that light was coming in along the edge of the door. You coughed twice, and lay back into the water. The saltwater washed into your crack, and a searing pain penetrated the core of your head. Flashes of pink and orange throbbed in your view in the dark. The individual crystalline shards of salt in the water sliced at your nerves, and you were certain that you'd either go insane or bleed out in the tank, and they'd find you dead in this pitch-black room.

After the pain subsided, some of the salt made its way into your urethra, and there was no way for you to stop the stinging itch. But, it felt oddly cathartic to let the water fill your ears, and as soon as it washed all the way to your ear canals, you remembered that you were supposed to have put in earplugs, so you had to get out, shower again, put the earplugs in, and settle back in the tank, let the water painfully wash into your crack again, you screaming this time, all of which made the possibility for any spiritual happening seem slim.

Now that you were fully wet, you were uncomfortably cold. Some of the outdoor air probably followed you into the tank. You lifted your legs, and you popped up to the surface with a *bloop*.

The weightlessness of your floating made you realize how much tension you carried in your legs. They were restless and tense from the years of holding you above the ground, resisting the pull of gravity.

You stretched your legs out all the way to your toes, and you tried to focus on the sensations in your body and to isolate and relax different muscle groups. You exhaled and released your stretch, and your legs twitched a few times. You stretched more, and breathed in deeply, and you pushed the inhaled air all the way to your belly, below even, to the tense joints in your hip flexors and to each of your tree-like legs.

You exhaled and relaxed again, and repeated this process several times. Stretch tall from the tips of your toes to the tips of your fingers above your head, why not? There's a lot of space in here. Letting your arms drift down like you were making a snow angel, you couldn't feel the edges of the tank. A pulse of adrenaline flashed through your body, and you quickly put your legs down to remind yourself that there were limits to the tank you were in. It had felt like you were somewhere else entirely.

You felt ridiculous. You let your legs float back up with the same *bloop*, and though you were calmer now, you began to suspect that maybe the something that you were supposed to find was just deep relaxation, and not a psychedelic voyage or a union with the source of consciousness. And, the fact that they charge you forty dollars just to float in a cold, dark room, not that you had to pay for it, but the principle… Well, might as well get your money's worth… Tom's money's worth.

You tried to meditate. What had Tom said? *Hmm* on the exhale, *saa* on the inhale? Or, was it the other way around?

You were able to focus on this longer than you'd

expected. In fact you were still doing it now. Each *saa* inhale seemed to expand your brain in your skull with a pleasant throb, and each *hmm* exhale released the whatever it was out of your brain and out of your nose. It felt like you were willing your brain to beat like a heart, filling it with energy and calmly sending that energy away, until a very soft, shallow *saa* inhale was released as an even softer *hmm* exhale that seemed to bring a little bit of you out with it.

You inhaled even more gently and felt that swelling energy again as you sipped the breath through your nose, and you waited a single beat before letting the *hmm* exhale be more of an escaping of air than a deliberate evacuation, like smoke effusing from the wick of a blown-out candle, and the exhale drained you out of your body for a moment, and another inhale washed you right back in. And, another exhale drained you out, and another inhale washed you back in, and this back-and-forth, in-and-out went on until it was clear there was an approaching transcendence of something or other, and it swelled as it approached, you drifting in and out of your body until it appeared that someone had opened the tank door, and a silhouette of a naked woman was framed in the doorway.

You could think only to cover your genitals, not that you and the mysterious intruder weren't already on the same playing field vulnerability-wise. She stepped into the tank and closed the door behind her. The flash of light from the outside was a disorienting contrast to the darkness of the tank, so her outline remained stained on your eyes. The woman said only, "*Shhh…*"

You felt her hand grab your foot, and she pulled you across the surface of the water, and she climbed on top of you and embraced you, laying her head on your chest. The only thing to do then was to wrap your arms around her and float.

You could tell she had firm breasts and an agreeable hip-to-waist ratio, your exploring hands discovered. The embrace was oddly not sexual, it was something else entirely, and you were surprised to find you didn't have an erection, and with that out of the picture it seemed like there was nothing else to do, and not just now, but ever again. You considered that having to die was not so bad

You felt her breath gently on your chest, little whispers of air. You matched her breath. Slowly. In and out. Her skin pressing against you seemed to draw you out of yourself all over again and let go of something you didn't know you were clinging to, something that had always been in the way, that stone pillar that was obstructing the view. And, it wasn't that your bodies became one, but more that you and she drifted away somewhere, and though you had never seen her face, you and she stared into each other's eyes, deliberately open to each other's gaze, saying nothing, and at last she opened her mouth to sing a single sad note that expressed the pain of trying to hold onto a reality that was swirling down the drain.

It made you feel like you were not just on a cold rock floating in space, but in a dream you woke up into, no longer trapped by the uncertainty of the world but entranced by the boundless expanse that makes—Wait! Where did she go? Her weight was gone from your chest.

You were severely disappointed to find that it had all been, you assumed, a dream. You felt that aching powerlessness that confirmed that your real life was always more disappointing than what you could imagine. But, it definitely was worth the forty dollars, you decided.

It was time to get out. You had had enough. You waved your hands in front of your face to appreciate one last moment of the total darkness, and when the salt water dripped down on your face and into your eyes, you laughed even though it stung, because the grunge guy had been right.

Chapter 4

After you drove back to Tom's, you planned on asking him for some gas money. Your tank was running low. You had a hard time locating the front door, so you walked around through the back again. Tom was sitting on the orange blob in the living room, leafing through a large stack of papers. He barked at you, "Where have you been? We've got work to do."

"The float appointment? You booked it for me."

"Yea? Well, you must be a really slow driver, because I've been waiting a long time."

"What? Did you want me to plow down the people in front of me?"

Tom recoiled in disgust. "That was hugely disturbing. Your head may be cracked, but your ego is alive and well, and in the way. And, frankly, you're really condescending. Anyway, your spiritual development begins now. Did you read the materials I gave you?"

"What materials?"

"I gave you a good two hundred and fifty dollars worth of spiritual literature. Did your brain fall out when you hit your head?"

"I have no memory of any materials being exchanged."

"In the hospital. I gave you the Bhagavad-Gita, the Tao Te Ching, the Bible, the Book of the Dead, and like twenty books of commentary. Christ."

"Did we go to the hospital?"

"How many times do we have to go over this?"

"Did we already go over this?"

"Yes. This gives me grave concerns for our arrangement. I cannot teach you if you cannot learn."

"I can learn, I promise."

"Can you? Can you even read?" He held up a paper to you. You strained to read the words typed on it, but a deep blur in your field of view obscured the words.

"Why is there so much required reading?"

"I've got to get the message across somehow. We haven't figured out telepathy yet."

"We could skip that, and actually get started with my journey."

"You wouldn't get any of my instruction, the references, *none* of the nuance."

You put a hand on your head. "Ow."

"What? What's happening?"

"When I think too hard, the crack starts to throb."

"How do you think I feel? You're asking me to condense an enormously contentious intellectual discourse spread across thousands of years of history and dozens of fields of thought into one speech."

"No one is asking you to do that."

"I'll do my best."

"This is worse than death."

"All of these major texts have something in common. You would know if you'd read any of them. They say things like 'the Tao that can be spoken is not the eternal Tao' and 'many know the techniques of Bhakti Yoga, and few ever achieve liberation with it' and 'those who know don't talk, and those who talk don't know' and all of these have something in common. Any guesses?"

"They're all impossible to understand?"

"It's easy for a Westerner to think that they indulge in tautologies, paradoxes, and contradictions because it's all just made-up, spiritual mumbo-jumbo, or outright wankery."

"But, how do you know it's not outright wankery?"

"Fair point. It can be helpful to start with our best Western equivalent."

"Hotels?"

"Come again?"

"Best Western…"

"Ugh," Tom grimaced. "Not funny. The seemingly confusing narratives and paradoxes they dole out in Eastern spiritual literature are not unlike those found in Western post-modern philosophy. But, the problem is that the goal of a lot of philosophers in the West is to determine 'the truth.' We have searched for 2,000 years now, and the only thing we know for certain is that we cannot know anything for certain, which leaves us exactly where we started—'it is a wise man who knows that he knows nothing,' which is a little contradiction in itself.

"But, even though we went through all that, we still haven't changed our goal, to determine the truth. And, since we frame the discussion more secularly, this produces a sad nihilism in the West, and we get caught in language traps, going crazy about what can be said and what can't be said and whether we can know what things can't be said, and if we can, how coherent is our view of what can't be said?"

"What the fuck are you talking about?"

"That our postmodern discourses' focus on that which cannot be said speaks volumes."

"Okay…"

"But, what if we changed the goal? What if we became less concerned with what *is* and became more concerned with what works? Or what *does*? What if we introduced metaphor, imagery, and symbolism into our discourses? What if we introduced… divinity? What if we made it a story?"

"If this is supposed to be a story, this is the most boring story I've ever heard."

"Whoa, hold the phone, bud. I've got a lot of material to cover before you can get out in the field."

"I'm pretty sure I get it. Westerners suck, Easterners rule."

"Not at all, Abraham. The importance of making your world view a story is that you can tell if you have changed. Progressed. Become enlightened." You sat staring at Tom, and you wiped the drool from your mouth. "In other words, without some concept of a story, you'll be stuck like this forever."

You shrieked in fear and straightened up.

"That's better. Also, it would be to throw the baby out with the bathwater if we ignored the better points of Western philosophy, like relativism—every single thing can never be known in and of itself because every thing depends on other things for its being, including you, which helps us arrive at the Buddhist concept of no-self…"

You yawned. Tom was getting into some technical shit, and you weren't sure you had the mental capacity for it. You looked at the counter-clockwise clock, and it took you a while, but you determined it was almost nine o'clock at night. You decided that first thing in the morning you'd get that gas money from Tom even if it meant taking money from his wallet.

Tom was still prattling on as he sat you in a chair in front of a mirror in the living room. "…and that's how you truly live presently in the moment. You say yes to what's in front of you, and assert something of your own." Tom was smiling warmly, proud of his emphatic conclusion. "Now, repeat back everything I just said to you."

"Uh…"

"Kidding. This takes time." He pulled out a pair of scissors and electric clippers.

"A lot of time apparently. You know, I'm not sure I want my hair that short."

"Oh, we're taking all of it off. I've just got to trim it short enough so we can shave it."

"No."

"What kind of spiritual journey do you think you signed up for, dude?" Tom asked curtly as he snipped off a huge tuft of your hair. You saw yourself in the mirror scowl at Tom, and he made eye contact with your reflection.

"Why do you get to have hair?"

The voice of the nameless general intelligence simulator filled the room, "It looks very nice, Mr.

Downey."

"Thanks for noticing."

"Did you program it to say that?"

"Neither here nor there. I get to have hair, one, because I have already become detached from the vanity of hair, and two, because there's not a crack on the back of my head worth examining."

You looked at yourself in the mirror with wide-eyed terror.

Tom's fingers explored the folds of the gauze, and he pinched a fold between his fingers, and pulled off an entire layer. You clasped your hands to your head to prevent it from unraveling any further.

"What are you doing, you maniac? I'm not supposed to take this off. Stuff might start leaking out."

"I promise, I will be absolutely careful."

"Why are you dying to see this so bad?"

"Are you familiar with trepanation?"

"No, what the fuck is trepanation?"

"It's a medical procedure where a small hole is drilled into your skull in order to relieve pressure on the brain. Some people think that you can use it to achieve a higher level of consciousness."

"Absolutely not." You backed away from Tom, who was still holding the end of your gauze wrap, so it looked like you were on a leash.

"It's just a theory."

"There is no way I'm letting you drill a hole through my head."

Tom stared at you for a moment. He threw his head back and started laughing. You did not find it amusing. "That would be highly unethical, and unsafe, and I would probably be prosecuted for doing it without a medical license. Besides, I don't have to. Your head is already cracked open."

You stared at him skeptically. He gave a little tug on the gauze, "Come. Sit back down." You slowly crossed to him and sat. "Good boy," he said cocking his head to the side and smiling at you in the mirror.

He unwound another layer, arriving at a spot wet with blood that had soaked through. Your wound tingled, and Tom's face seemed to warp and bend in the reflection in the mirror, but even through the oscillations, you could see excitement and awe in it. The light in the room grew very bright.

You heard the crinkling of the gauze that was stiff with dried blood as Tom pulled it away from the layer beneath. At last, Tom removed the last layer of gauze, and squinted at the tangled mess of blood, hair, and skin that had wrinkled up and away from the crack. After clearing away the clumps of hair, he stared into your crack with orgasmic fascination and slack-jawed wonder.

He grabbed the scissors, and gingerly gathered a clump of hair that was wet with blood. He grimaced slightly as he snipped at the clump.

But, he said, "So, where were we?"

"Ugh…" you moaned, still distrustful of Tom's prying fingers.

"Something about… Oh! Have you gotten laid yet?"

"I've been floating all day."

"That's no excuse. What exactly are you doing when you approach these women?"

"I just introduce myself, I guess…" you lied.

Tom had already launched into a diatribe about approaching women as he continued grabbing handfuls of your hair and cutting at them roughly with the scissors. It turned out that spirituality was only a small part of his oeuvre. He had quite the narrative of seduction and a huge methodology and discourse on what's going on when people engage in what he referred to as "the game."

In fact, a great portion of his speech was dedicated to explaining why a lot of other methodologies and discourses were shortsighted and incoherent. He eventually mentioned animal instincts, primal urges, domination and submission, and the penis and vagina as classic signs of presence and absence. But, none of it really cohered into anything meaningful for you.

Tom must have noticed the lost look on your face. He shook your shoulders. "Are you getting any of this?"

"Yea…"

"Then repeat back to me what I just said."

You smiled.

"Seriously, this time."

"…to get laid, you basically find the object of your desire, and try not to come on too strong."

"Object of desire? Abraham, this troubles me deeply. Do you know what it means to actually objectify a woman?"

"Treat her like a piece of furniture?"

"No. Not that kind of object. To objectify a woman is to turn her into a pursuit, a task to be conquered, a symbol of your transformation. You don't think of women that way, do you?"

"Of course not."

"Good. If so, you'd be in deeper trouble than I thought."

He grabbed one last clump of hair and cut it off. He pulled a saffron robe over your head and shoulders, and an electric buzz told you that he had turned on the clippers, and he proceeded to remove the rest of your hair, being ever so careful to shave up to but not into the crack in the back of your head. You watched his reflection in the mirror gaze at the crack with wonder, and he lightly traced his finger from the crack's start, the top of the left side of your neck, to its end, on the crown of your head. Tom let his finger slip into the crack and you heard a slurp, and a searing cold pain flashed through your body.

"Easy now!" you cried.

"Sorry. Hold still."

He slid his finger in the crack once again, and this time, he wiggled it, and you felt the crack open and close slightly, which sent lightning strikes of pain into the center of your head, and the wetness of inside your skull slurped and squished, and everything in your vision flickered. The individual objects that you saw before you in the mirror—the couch, the ladder to the loft you'd been sleeping in, the granite coffee table, the TV, you, Tom, each individual garment you were wearing, the eyes on your face and Tom's face, and both of your noses and mouth and hands—began to seem to sink into themselves, as though each thing was retreating into some withdrawn hole within. With another wiggle of Tom's finger inside the crack in your head, each object in the room began to expand out of that same supposed hole. Tom nudged his finger deeper, everything went black, with the sound of radio static in the background.

You came to, and after you realized what was happening, you lurched away from Tom once more.

"Okay, I'm done. I need some gauze right now," you demanded.

Tom nodded and left the room silently and returned with gauze. He handed it to you, and you proceeded to wrap it tightly around your head. Tom had opened his wallet, and he pulled four one-hundred-dollar bills out of his wallet. "That should help you get through the next few days. You may go."

Chapter 5

You ran out the back door and around the house to the front driveway. You started your car, and stepped on the gas. Before long, you were driving down the famous Sunset Blvd. There were surprisingly few cars out. The lights on the individual storefronts blended in your peripheral vision into one continuous strip of light as you zoomed by, like the discrete frames on a filmstrip played as a presently unfolding movie. The street lights left long trails behind them like they were shooting stars and the moon sank in the sky, leaving a smear of yellow-orange light behind it, until it looked like it was about to crash into your car. You screamed and covered your face, but at the moment of impact, everything went back to normal.

You heard a dinging sound and thought your mind was playing tricks on you, but you saw that your fuel indicator light was blinking on the dashboard. You were on empty. You drove toward the closest gas station, but your car sputtered to a halt. You slammed your hand on the steering wheel in anger.

You had to push your car ten blocks to a gas station, and after several days of gloomy weather, the sun had finally come out, so you were drenched in sweat, and it washed into your eyes and into the wound on the back of your head, which stung terribly. There was no shoulder on the road, so you had to push your car in the right lane in traffic. Drivers in cars behind you shouted obscenities and honked at your slow pace, angrily jerking their steering wheels to speed past you. A particularly enraged man in his late forties threw a bottle of green Gatorade at your head as he passed. It hit you right in the crack in the back of your head, making everything explode into a white light, and you collapsed, and if you hadn't scurried out of the way, your car would have rolled backwards over you. Some of the Gatorade dripped into your mouth, and it seemed like a new flavor.

You finally got to the gas station. You bought a green Gatorade while the tank was getting filled, and you were amazed at how much that cheered you up. It was like your brain was a shriveled raisin, and the Gatorade turned it back into a ripe, juicy grape.

Your joy faded as you slowly began to realize that Tom's spiritual instruction was turning out to be harder on your head than you'd anticipated.

But, where else could you go? You'd basically be homeless without Tom. Who else would have you with that crack on the back of your head, which was throbbing the more stressed you got? You panicked as your vision got blurry. You never should have let Tom unwrap the gauze.

The pressure swelled immensely in your skull. You had to do something to calm yourself. You pulled to the side of the gas station and turned off your car.

You closed your eyes, and as you did, the sticky sugars of the Gatorade that had dried on your eyelids gave a fair amount of resistance. You tried meditating. You breathed a *hmm* exhale and a *saa* inhale back and forth for some time. It had not struck you in the float lab to experiment with how you said the mantra in your head. You played with stretching the words of the mantra out for as long as you could breathe, a long *hmmmmm* exhale and an even longer *saaaaaa* inhale, then you did the opposite until the *hmm* and the *saa* were choppy, digital flashes in your head.

Then you tried changing the volume with which you thought them, exhaling a very loud *HMM* and inhaling a louder *SAAA,* until you were screaming both in your head. Then you made them both so quiet that they were only whispers, and then completely silent, as though you were only mouthing them in your head. To your amazement, you began to calm down.

You reached a state of mind that was pure imagery, forms of objects that morphed continuously, never resting in any one state, until the mood of all of them grew darker, and more violent. You grew fearful as barking dogs morphed into caged apes with foot-long fangs that dripped blood, and the drops rained down on people, seared by the steaming liquid, and their skin sloughed off, and their skeletal remains piled into a heap which caught fire and smoldered down to dull ash, and the passing wind lifted the ash and blew it to a moonlit graveyard, and all of the plots were open and empty, and a bored groundskeeper checked his watch, and looked to you and shrieked and clasped his hands around your throat, and everything disappeared, and you were immersed in darkness.

You were in such a subtle level of consciousness that you were no longer thinking, even your *hmm-saa* mantra had faded, until you were experiencing only the weight of your body sitting in your car, and even that seemed to grow lighter until if felt like you had been lifted out of your seat. It felt like there was still one more thing in your way, you weren't sure what, but it seemed like if you could let go just a little bit more—*bing bing!*

A text had come in, and you were delivered back to the dull reality of your sticky face and hot car. It was from Tom. It read, "Check out this band at The Fighter Pilot tomorrow night. It's a hip dive in Los Feliz. Bartenders are smokin'." That bastard. If only he'd known how close you were to transcendence.

You bought a bottle of water and poured it over your face in the parking lot of the gas station to wash the sugar off. A lady who was walking past you muttered, "Classy." You restrained yourself from throwing the empty bottle at her.

You got in your car and started cruising, and after you remembered to take down the convertible top, you felt a whole lot better. You were in Los Angeles with hundreds of dollars in your pocket, and no one was there to stop you. You floored the gas through every yellow light and you weaved in and out of traffic.

After you'd had your fun, you slowed down, parked, and entered one of the little storefronts on the Strip. You were absolutely present in the space of whatever coffee shop, restaurant, bar, or boutique you walked into. You could not tell which because your vision had completely lost the distinction between individual objects. You could not see anything's surface, only the ether that everything floated in, which was not a sight at all, nor totally black either. It was mostly a sense that the world of objects had been painted on, and could just as easily be washed away. Good thing you had pulled over.

But, that moment passed. And, after a while, your vision went back to mostly normal. Individual objects still had blurry edges, and the lights seemed a little blown out, but you still felt present and increasingly alert. You discovered that you had entered some sort of gothic novelty shop. There were stuffed crows mounted on gnarled logs; dead bats floating in some liquid in sealed mason jars; swords with ornately designed handles, their blades wedged into the notches in their display stands; and a whole lot of what looked like ceremonial garments: shawls, gowns, tunics, leather-strapped vests, and even footwear, all decorated with skulls and tombstones.

There was a young woman behind the checkout counter with large gauges stretching out her earlobes, a septum piercing, and a tattoo that said something in Latin beneath her left eye. The top of her head was shaved but the sides were long, and a few dreadlocks were hanging off the back of her head. You didn't know how long she'd been staring at you. You gasped.

"Can I help you?" she asked sweetly.

"Just browsing."

"The bats are half off."

"Good to know."

She continued staring at you, not saying anything, so you turned around to pretend to root through a spinning rack of thongs that were made of barbed wire. You figured you'd look for another minute and then casually leave, just like a normal person having a normal night in a death store.

"Are you alright?"

"Yea, just a little tired."

"You're not driving are you?"

"Nope, just out for a stroll."

"What happened to your head?"

"I don't remember."

"Bummer. Have you seen a doctor?"

"No... Yes... I've got a guy taking care of it."

You rushed out of the store and onto the sidewalk. Was it a coincidence that you'd wandered into a death shop? Maybe you were dead: your mind was coping with fading away.

That's what it had felt like anyway. That you were caught in an afterlife and all of this was supposed to teach you something—Tom's antics, the woman who had appeared in the float tank, the crack in your head. You felt the doom of the simultaneous certainties that everything in your reality had eternal significance and that it would all be gone before you had time to decode it.

After hyperventilating for a few minutes with your heart pounding in your chest, you realized that if death had found you, it was taking its sweet time with finishing you off. And, if the objects around you were a façade, that could be comfortably lived with until it proved to cause problems. You put the car in drive and entered the street.

Maybe Tom would be able to help you after all. The meditation had done something, and you were sure that the more compelling aspect of his instruction would emerge after he finished sharing the boring details.

Tom had such a way with words. He had already talked your ear off without ever stuttering or pausing to think. You felt guilty that you had doubted him earlier, and you planned to make it up to him by trying harder than ever to go on your transformative journey. Surely that would impress him, and show him that you were serious about getting better.

You were deep into your daydream about how noble it was to have such a practical plan for yourself, when the sky started glowing deep red. Your vision began to blur and focus, back and forth, slowly at first, but then in rapid succession. And, you saw what appeared to be a hand reaching out of the sky at you, and for an instant, you were disoriented because you didn't realize that you had been staring at the western setting sun. You momentarily lost your perception of up and down and side to side, and—*honk!*

The road you were on had turned into a highway that brought you between two huge mountain crests, and cars were whizzing past you at eighty miles per hour, and their drivers were screaming obscenities out the window, and the highway dipped into a long, downward slope. You held onto the steering wheel for dear life and tried to merge toward the nearest exit.

When you exited you were alarmed that the road looped around and spat you out in front of a fork in the road, and each side of the fork split into another. You careered around a driver who slammed on the brakes without warning, and a cyclist swerved into your lane. A huge pothole in the road sent a jolt through your car, and the crack on the back of your head throbbed, which cast the trees around you into a scintillating flash.

You turned into a residential area, and drove at twenty-four miles per hour, just to savor the calmer speed limit. It started to rain. The houses around you had peeling paint, and a few of their storm drains were missing, so the rain brought a slick, dirty wash over their walls, windows, and doors. It actually looked like the rain was washing the paint right off the houses. At the end of the street was a huge wall beneath the interstate. In front of it, there were more than a few tents in clusters on the sidewalk. Trash swirled in the pooled rainwater that slowly drained down the sewer. A white Ferrari sped past you, and the woman driving it winked at you.

After driving for a while, you arrived at Tom's house, and after you parked and entered through the back door, you realized that you were absolutely exhausted. You climbed up the ladder to the loft, and settled into the king-sized bed, but Tom called from somewhere in the house, "Would you mind sleeping in the sleeping bag? Blood is hard to wash out of white linens." You groaned and rolled off the bed onto the sleeping bag. "Thanks, bro."

Part 2

Baby Doll

Chapter 6

You awoke to your phone's *bing bing*. It was from Tom, reminding you about the punk show. The counterclockwise-moving clock that you had gotten better at deciphering revealed that you had apparently slept all day.

You drove to The Fighter Pilot and parked a few blocks away. Inside, there was a WWI biplane replica suspended from the ceiling, and the waitresses wore air force jumpsuits. Tom had not been joking. Every one of them was stunning, and you stammered, unable to look them in the eye as you ordered a Bloody Mary.

There was a stage that was done up like an old USO show, with American flags and red-white-and-blue decorations everywhere, and an old-fashioned microphone right in the middle of the stage.

Tonight, a woman walked out on the stage, dressed up like a doll with tight, curling-ironed hair, and painted-on freckles, dimples, and rosy cheeks. She curtseyed and shyly thanked everyone for coming and paused, before singing a single sad note that seemed to reach into your soul.

As her sad note rang out, she allowed it to turn into vibrato. Another figure entered the stage dressed as a doll, but he had hairy legs, and a thicker frame, and on his face was a mask with the same tight, curling-ironed curls and painted-on freckles, dimples, and rosy cheeks; but he had drumsticks in his hand and as he sat down, he stomped on the bass pedal in no rhythm whatsoever, and the woman, still holding her long note, raised a middle finger to the audience and proceeded to put it in her mouth and down her singing throat, and she gagged and vomited down her white dress and the drummer crashed on the cymbals, and the woman lifted her barf-covered dress over her head, and she wore nothing beneath, but the word *fuck* was written in Sharpie above her navel. She writhed on the ground in her upturned dress, which was like a straightjacket around her flailing, barfy body.

After she had finished flailing and the drummer had all but destroyed his drum set, they lay breathing heavily on the ground, and she rose from the floor and pulled her dress back down and smoothed it against her legs. She wiped her face with her hand, missing a chunk of puke that stuck to her cheek, and whispered into the microphone, "Fuck you very much."

After the show, she walked through the audience and greeted her friends warmly, thanking them for coming, and hugging them as though she were not still covered in puke. You approached her, anxiety swelling in you, until you looked right in her eyes and said… nothing for a few moments because she stared right back at you completely patient and open to your dumbstruck gaze.

She grabbed your hand and shook it, and she said under her breath, "Say your name."

"I'm Abraham."

"Say it like an introduction."

"Abraham. I'm Abraham. Hello, I am Abraham."

"Lovely. I am Baby Doll. It's a tragedy to meet you."

"Likewise."

"Come smoke hydroponic marijuana with me."

You were not thrilled at the prospect of getting stoned with this spectacular woman. Girl. Baby Doll. You were weak in the knees and stuttering in her presence even without the paranoid stupor marijuana could induce. After a few hits, it would be difficult to do anything at all, let alone engage her in any sort of... What could you have to offer that would excite someone like Baby Doll?

She had already been leading you by the hand to the back room of The Fighter Pilot, the "green room" it might have been called if it were not occupied by storage bins and cardboard boxes full of plastic airliner nameplates with those gold-tipped wings with no names on them yet, and a yellow bucket and mop and a few spray bottles and paper towels.

All of this would have led you to believe that it was a storage closet were it not for the throw pillows that covered the floor, and a coffee table that had a picture of a cigarette in a red circle with a slash through it and carved around that was a circle and slash through it, the implication being that not smoking was not allowed. There would be no way you could decline.

On one of the pillows was the drummer who had removed his mask and revealed himself to be Tom Downey himself. He smiled and flourished his hands.

"Surprise!"

"I never would have guessed."

"How did we do?"

"It was horrifying."

"Oh, I'm so glad you thought so!" said Baby Doll.

You felt the need to occasionally direct your attention to her while you were talking to Tom.

"Let us break bud."

"I suppose we could," you said

"Isn't he perfect?"

"He certainly is," said Tom. You'd never been accused of being perfect before.

They broke up some of the greenest, fluffiest marijuana buds you'd ever seen, and they loaded it in a little vaporizer that was shaped like a V-2 rocket with a rubber hose with a mouthpiece at the end coming out of the top. There was a digital plate near the afterburners that showed the temperature readout.

They insisted that you take the first hit, and you reluctantly accepted the hose, and the digital readout reached 315 and it shook as though it were about to blast off when you inhaled, and you mentally intoned *saa* out of habit. You were filled with a delightful anxiety like a tickle of adrenaline, as you exhaled and thought *hmm.* You passed the hose to Baby Doll, who gave you suggestive eyebrows while she pulled deeply and passed the hose.

The pleasant tickle you had gave way to a thorough panic that you tried to keep hidden. You were the odd one out in this group of punks, or whatever Baby Doll and Tom were supposed to be. You felt pretty silly in your gray sweat pants and Gatorade-and-blood-stained white t-shirt. You realized you had not changed clothes since moving to LA.

Everyone had become silent. There was nothing particularly expectant or awkward about the silence either, just a pause to let everyone have their moment alone, the comfort with which animals seem to lounge around each other without feeling the need to make noise… But, it had been quite a long time now. And though it was peaceful, you absolutely couldn't take it anymore, asking in a tone that surprisingly concealed your panic, "So?"

Silence fell again. Tom seemed comfortable sitting there staring. Baby Doll pulled you close to her and lay down on your chest. The smell of the barf on her dress was pretty strong, so you breathed through your mouth and tried to ignore it. You worked up the courage to comb your fingers through her hair.

After a while, Baby Doll suggested going home. You followed her car in your car, swerving wildly in and out of the lane because of the beers and the weed, not to mention the crack on the back of your head. Baby Doll pulled into Tom's driveway. They must be neighbors. That's how they knew each other, you concluded. But, then the car pulled up to the gate in front of Tom's house. You rolled down your window.

"Do you live here?"

"I sure do," called Baby Doll out of her window.

"You live with Tom?"

"Duh," said Tom without looking at you.

That meant you and Baby Doll had been in the same house, probably at the same time. But, Tom's house was big enough that you could have been in there for weeks and never crossed paths.

Baby Doll led you and Tom to the white cube

on the western end of the house that was illuminated by light that changed colors. She located the front door easily and led you inside the hallway of doors that were all different. Baby Doll approached the enormous steel door that had scared you earlier, and she grabbed the huge dial on the front and steered it like a brave sailor at the wheel of a ship, powerfully navigating the treacherous seas. She collapsed and laughed to herself. The door remained closed.

She led you and Tom away from the giant door with the dial, but you couldn't help but glance at it with some suspicion that it might hide something terrible.

At last, you entered what you could only call the sitting room, or one of the sitting rooms. You had passed several others before arriving at this one. But, you had never been to this particular room. It was full of psychotherapy chairs. Baby Doll held her skirt down as she slid into one and got comfortable. Tom sat as well, but he didn't have the courtesy to hold his skirt down. You looked away swiftly and settled into a chair yourself. Baby Doll whistled as though calling for a dog, and the nameless general intelligence simulator's voice filled the house.

"Yes?" the voice answered.

"Three head sets, please."

Mechanical arms descended from the ceiling. Each had a set of goggles and earphones hanging from them.

"What's going on?" you asked.

"VR," said Baby Doll with a smirk, and she put on the goggles and her earphones.

"Tom's Secret Cocktail is under your chair if you

want," and she pulled a little plastic baggie full of white powder out from beneath her chair. She put a little handful in her mouth and threw the bag and rubbed her hands together excitedly.

Tom had already put on his headset. He emptied the entire bag of his Secret Cocktail into his mouth. He lifted his goggles to search for the bag Baby Doll had thrown, and he emptied it into his mouth too. He smiled at you mischievously and held a finger to his mouth and mouthed *shhh*.

"Space?" Baby Doll offered.

"Farm?" Tom asked.

"Are you fucking kidding me?"

"I like those little chickens," said Tom, pouting.

"Boring. Space is the obvious answer," said Baby Doll, and you giggled to hide your terror. You were still blasted from that rocket marijuana vaporizer and now you were expected to step into virtual reality on Tom's Secret Cocktail, into space, no less.

You clicked a button on the VR goggles that turned them off as you put them over your eyes. If Baby Doll or Tom peeked out of their goggles, they would think you were on drugs and soaring through space just like them. In reality, you could take this as an opportunity to get some sleep. But, your mind wandered in excitement. There you were, sharing in a genuine experience with what was shaping up to be a group of friends.

Chapter 7

The better you got to know Baby Doll, the more hopelessly enamored you became with her mysterious aura. She could stick her tongue up her nostril. She also frequently pretended to be a pirate, squaring up in front of you with a menacing grin with a curled finger for her hook that she'd brandish at you before tackling you to the ground and declaring herself pirate king of the land, with an imaginary flag stabbed into you to boot. What a punk. This went on until one day you passed out from being tackled too hard or from neglecting the crack on your head.

After that, the two of you never did anything physical except for her laying her head on your chest and your wrapping your arms around her, not even caressing her most of the time. It was as though she grew very tired when you were around and she had to catch up on sleep, and you could always use a nap, so after a little small talk, her usually dominating the conversation with aggressive histrionics, you'd settle into the usual pose and drift off together.

When she was wrapped around you, an acceptance of death crept over you. Just holding her balanced out the fact that all of your earthly efforts would eventually be erased.

She cradled your bald head, careful to avoid touching the bleeding crack.

"What do you even get out of this?"

"This right here." She lifted her head and punched your chest. "Your chest is nearly perfectly head-shaped. It's the best sanctuary for my troubled head I've found so far."

"I see," you wheezed, pretending she hadn't knocked the wind out of you.

"And, you're pretty easy on the eyes."

"What do you mean?"

"Has anyone ever told you that before? You are beautiful, Abraham. You are a true work of art. But, there's a lot of negative energy in you. So, I've taken it upon myself to work it out."

"Looks like you've just been lying there."

"Anything more intense than that might split you in two."

"Try me."

"You asked for it."

Baby Doll lifted her head and raised your shirt so that she could place her palm between your nipples and she pressed down and released and pressed down again and released again, searching.

"There it is," she said. She made small circles on your chest, and you felt underneath the pressure of her hand a warmth that woke a pain that had been hiding deep inside of you, and in the flesh under your rib cage, a poised resistance to the outside world. When Baby Doll found it, she began the process of kneading it away, massaging it and finding the knots and the stitches you'd been harboring, and she worked her thumbs into the spaces in between your ribs, softening the meat, and as she worked you realized you were crying from what her digging unearthed. When she reached your solar plexus it became too much and you grabbed her hands to stop her. She lay back on your chest as you sobbed, but through your tears you felt a relief spread through you from letting them fall and from the fact that Baby Doll did not condemn or encourage your tears. She merely accepted your blubbering, snotty quivers that shook her resting head, which made the act of crying seem as quotidian as eating or getting dressed.

You wrapped your arms around her and rolled her over so that you could lie on her chest, and she said, "Don't get any ideas," but you had already lifted her shirt and put a hand between her breasts to release that same tension that you were sure lurked within her somewhere and she laughed and said, "Let me know if you find anything." Sure enough, her chest gave way with the pressure of your hand, and the meat between her ribs was soft. All the while, she looked back at you unblinking and patient for you to learn that the deep pain you carried around did not reside in her body, and surprising to you was that none of the aforementioned interaction had been sexual, but now with her shirt above her breasts, and that calm accepting gaze, you had to have her, to touch her and go inside of her, have traditional intercourse and get her pregnant. You put your hand over her breast and kissed her mouth, but her lips did not move. You kissed her again, and she smiled and said, "If you need to come, go ahead, but I won't have anything to do with it." So, you rolled off of her and pulled down your pants and began to masturbate to her as she looked into your eyes, but you stopped, suddenly feeling ridiculous at the thought of you with your pants around your knees trying to pleasure yourself to a half-naked woman who, although she was a few feet away from you, seemed like she was miles away, in outer space maybe, looking down on all of this, dispassionately.

You pulled up your pants and pulled her shirt back down, and you lay down and she climbed back on top of you and placed her head back on your chest. She rose for a moment and tapped your erection that was tenting up your pants. She said, "Are you sure you don't want to take care of this?"

"I'll ignore it if you will."

She smiled and said, "Already have been."

Not long after that you made an excuse to leave.

The next time you saw her, she gave no hint that she paid any mind to the incident the other day. In fact, she paid no mind to you at all. She and Tom were both sitting on the psychotherapy chairs wearing VR goggles, and seemingly gazing into each other's eyes, and Baby Doll was playing with a piece of Tom's thinning, gray hair. They hadn't even noticed your entrance, until you cleared your throat.

Baby Doll raised her VR goggles, and Tom Downey did the same. When he saw it was you, he smiled, did an ironic sign of the cross, and put a handful of his Secret Cocktail onto his tongue. You looked to the novelty counterclockwise-spinning clock in Tom's living room, and you saw that the hands were now moving clockwise.

Tom said, "Abraham. Baby Doll told me

everything."

"She did?"

"Yes. And, I'm not pleased."

"I didn't mean to do anything wrong," you pleaded.

"Relax, bro. I know going into VR can be scary, but you need to do it."

"Oh. I don't think I could..."

Tom Downey became voluble and impassioned.

He said, "This is the best time to be alive." Tom was pacing and gesticulating, and quickly got out of breath. "It's all right here," he said, holding up the VR goggles like a priest holding a consecrated host. "This is our access to the world of the real. This is enlightenment at the press of a button. Transcendence on demand. The Buddhists for millennia have taught that the world is an illusion, a synthesis of attachments that hide the nothingness beneath, but the West has managed to hot-wire the whole process. Because what do you get when you step willingly into a world that admits that it is fake? What do you find when the space and time around you give full disclosure that they are constructs erected to make sense of an uncertain world? What do we have when we accept that our environment is false? Literally just ones and zeros organized into sense and put on a screen? Abraham. Not rhetorical questions."

"Shit, I don't know."

"Freedom. Transcendence. Godhood. The experience of a Bodhisattva with all the detachment of an audience with popcorn and Coke at the movies. It's a lie we step into in order to exist in a world we know is absolutely reducible to rules, computerized sense, and the best 3D headphones that money can buy."

There was something inspiring about the way he spoke with passion you had never been able to muster since clunking your head, but you also thought that Tom had lost his mind on his Secret Cocktail. Also, his apparent enlightenment hadn't taught him much about how people dress in LA. But, you looked down and saw that you hadn't changed your clothes in what must have been weeks now, and you sniffed the collar of your shirt. It smelled like old lettuce.

"But, it's literally a fake world," you protested.

"But, it gives us exactly what we need for a discourse to develop. Reducible terms. Boundaries. A horizon to play within. You're still trying to peek over the horizon and language prevents us from doing that."

"I've never tried to peek over anything."

Tom frowned. He rushed out the door, claiming that he had been inspired to work on a new VR experience. Apparently, he was a coder too, and Baby Doll informed you that most of the experiences that she had trekked into were creations of Tom's. And, since that was the case, you became even more threatened by him.

Chapter 8

Tom emerged inspired into the living room, "I could kick myself for not thinking of it earlier!" Baby Doll lifted her head from your chest. "We have to start with much more basic skills. Communication. Emotions. Eye contact. Listening. Patience. I have just the thing."

"What?"

"We're going to do improv."

"Come again?"

"Improvisational scenic theater."

"Is that where you play pretend?"

"No. Well, kinda."

"That sounds hard." You cradled your head.

"Improv will change it all for you, buddy. Imagine an experience that openly admits it's pretend in order to create authenticity."

"I can't."

"Exactly. Because you haven't learned the rules. I don't want to liken improv to a religion because I'm sure your stance on that would be bleak." Tom waited for your reaction, but the words didn't seem to have been received. "But, improv is a cult of sorts, but one that is so pure that you can forgive yourself for getting swept away with it."

"I don't know, Tom. I'm afraid it might irritate my crack."

"If improv can't save you, you are certainly doomed."

You barrel-rolled sideways, rolling you and Baby Doll over so that you were on top, and you shot up and snapped to attention. She laughed wildly.

Tom said, "Improv is all about the rule of 'Yes, and.' First, you say 'Yes.' 'Yes' to your surroundings, 'Yes' to your scene partner, and 'Yes' to yourself. Radical acceptance of the present moment. For better or worse. But, you can't just leave it there. You have to say, 'Yes, *and*.' Assert something of your own. Put yourself out there. Get your two cents in. You say 'Yes, and' to your life, and you can confront it head-on, but you don't just 'Yes, and' with your words."

"Then how in the heck am I supposed to do it?"

"You 'Yes, and' with your attitude."

You stared blankly back at Tom.

"You're off to a terrible start. Baby Doll, initiate a scene with Abraham." Baby Doll approached you and pretended to type digits on your chest with her finger, silently mouthing *boop boop boop* as she did. She said, "Access granted," in a robotic voice and mimed opening a door and reaching into your chest. She pulled out an imaginary rifle, and aimed it at Tom. "Put your hands up. This improv lesson is being held hostage." She flourished her hands and smirked.

Clapping and cheering, Tom said, "Baby *Doll*! Those were very strong choices. Excellent work. Smart guy, we need you to make a few more choices."

"What kind of choices should I make?"

"It's best to make emotionally authentic choices."

"That's out of my control."

"You're thinking about it too hard."

You rubbed your head, saying, "I don't think so."

Tom stared at you intently for a moment and his mouth was slightly agape. He was looking at you as though you were an inanimate object, taking his time to inspect your face. "So, I think I know what your problem is. You are putting the whole truth-and-authenticity thing on a pedestal. It isn't this transcendent thing out of our experience. It's something we access all the time. Through improv.

"In real life, once we recognize that we are living authentically and that we're lost in our actions and emotions, we aren't living truthfully and authentically any more. We remove authenticity with that observation. So, how do we tap into that truth without freaking out and pissing all over it with excitement? We acknowledge that the tools we used to get there are imperfect. So, to drive that point home, we—" Tom darted out of the room for a moment, and he returned hoisting a large, green military-issue bag over his shoulder, "—are going to improvise—" and he dumped out the contents of the bag "—with puppets."

You managed to truthfully and authentically express your dissatisfaction with the prospect of playing with puppets, without having to say anything at all. You picked up a puppet, glaring at Tom. You put your hand in it and you said in a terrible, high-pitched character voice, "There's a pain in my ass."

"No jokes," shouted Tom. "Live in the moment. Respond. Make a decision."

"I'm trying, but you keep stopping me."

"I was under the impression that we are

responsible for our own lives. Baby Doll, is there anyone stopping you from living authentically?"

"Nope!"

"Yea, me neither. Maybe Abraham is different. Maybe everybody else has it wrong. Try it again."

You stood dumbfounded.

"How about you give her something to work with. So far, you've established yourself as a needy nobody floating around doing nothing of consequence. Who wants to hang out with a needy nobody?"

Tom immediately regretted asking you for anything because you threw the hand puppet on the ground, and you started flailing around, gyrating and seizing, making awful sounds. You started grunting, and you crawled around and hooted like a chimp.

Tom let you tire yourself out, and you lay breathing heavily on the ground, and when he was certain that you were done, he said softly, "And, Scene."

He stepped over you and picked up the puppet you had thrown. He gingerly brushed the dust off of its plastic, yellow hairs, and she put it on, and made the mouth of it talk, saying, "I'm not difficult. I'm a puppet. There's no trick. Nothing you have to be in on to operate me. Children do it, for gods' sakes. So, if you can't make me work… yikes. I don't know what I can do for you. I am just a puppet," and he dropped the puppet, "and, an improv coach. And, a three-time winner of Improv Thunder Dome. I can do my best to help you play pretend, but psychoanalysis is not my specialty."

"Thanks," you said bitterly.

"But," he said, spinning around to face you. "It is in my realm to discuss your little chaotic freak-out in terms of improvisation. That you frantically lashed out like a crazy person, speaks volumes about what you will do when given the absolute freedom to do anything. But, anything wasn't good enough so you tried to go all the way to infinity.

"The problem is that you cannot practically reach infinity. You have to work within your limits. And, on a stage the limits are the most freeing—your imagination and your body. But that was… predictable, boring, cringe-worthy, and… pathetic."

Baby Doll nodded.

"See? You don't have to try to go where the sun don't shine, why not explore the infinity that exists between zero and one? An infinite series of nuance and subtlety in the realm of the possible."

You had already blacked out from moving around too much, so most of Tom's analysis wasn't received. He only stopped talking when he realized that you had been drooling on the carpet.

Days later, Tom had returned to lecturing, "There exist spiritual reflections of yourself everywhere. You reflect the universe around you, and it reflects you back."

"Are you pulling my leg?"

"No. There are infinite instances of it: our entire existence, in fact, is an infinite series of reflections, microcosms, simulacra… 'As above, so below,'" Tom said, as though that had clarified matters for you.

"I'm not buying it."

"It is! You are used to being egocentric, so you don't think of yourself as a reflection. You think of yourself as a subject that can dominate the world around you. But, there are larger forces at play that grant us our seeming central placement in the universe."

"Yea? Well, I think you're egocentric."

"It's not an attack. It's your general human grasping for power, shrinking from pain. Everyone has an ego. Yours is just especially in the way."

You pouted and fumed. "You're ruining this beautiful day."

"See? This is what I'm talking about. You childishly shrink from anything that you don't like."

"I don't care. I want to go outside and play."

"Aren't you a little old for that? How old are you?"

You shrugged.

"A man your approximate age should learn delayed gratification." Tom lit a joint that he had withdrawn from some mysterious fold in his saffron robe. "Your unwillingness to work is," he inhaled deeply on the joint, and it crackled a little, and holding the smoke in his lungs he wheezed, "really pathetic," and exhaled, coughing.

You whimpered and whined. You finally shouted, "I want to go to the beach!"

"We have to—" Tom was struck with an epiphany. "The beach! Yes, we're going to the beach. Baby Doll! Come! Let's leave immediately."

It took a moment for you to realize that you had gotten what you wanted. You jumped up with glee and tripped and fell onto the ground.

The three of you drove to the beach in Tom's white Ford Bronco with surfboards bungee-corded to the roof. You had wanted to take the Ferrari, but Tom meanly pointed out, "Only two seats, Abe. Also, I want to keep a low profile."

You arrived at a quiet cove south of Malibu, and Baby Doll opened the door and jumped out of the car before Tom had come to a complete stop. She sprinted across the bike path, into the sand and shoreline. Tom sauntered slowly to the sand and spread out a towel to lie on while you started to make your way far away from him, toward some jagged rocks that were wet with the tide. They held pools in their crevasses that had trapped urchins, anemones, starfish, and hermit crabs. You crouched and climbed on all fours, scaling the rocks like an animal.

"Hello," Baby Doll's voice emerged from behind you.

You gave a startled glance at her, and she laughed at you. She climbed onto the rocks and stood tall with one foot up on a rock, gazing out at the water with her hand above her brow to block the sun. She said nodding, "Yup. It's an ocean."

You crawled to her, and she petted your head.

She looked deep into your eyes and you saw that she was concerned about something. She said, as though she could no longer bear waiting, "Do you think you would ever drink blood?"

After careful consideration, you said, "Repeat the question."

She did.

"No."

"Why not?"

"Seems unnatural and gross."

"But, what if you were raised in a culture that drank blood? For ritual purposes maybe?"

"I guess, in that case, it could be acceptable. If it was only a little bit of blood, maybe."

"See?"

"See what?"

"It's not this crazy thing."

"Still think it's gross. But, I guess, as long as everyone involved is okay with it…"

Baby Doll looked away. She stood, and without warning, dove into the water.

You shot upright uneasily to see where she had jumped, but nothing emerged from the water after her initial splash. You panicked and edged toward the water, then backed away in fear, as it appeared the splash was coming to swallow you. It would be best to alert Tom that Baby Doll was drowning or drowned or dead.

You sprinted on the sand, which was no easy task, and your mouth became dry at your body's sudden exertion. Out of breath and delirious, you got to Tom, who had been lazily setting up an umbrella. You managed to say, "Baby Doll"—heaving—"Water—"

And, you collapsed next to Tom's towel, howling.

"Abraham?" Baby Doll's voice said.

You looked up in disbelief, with sand stuck to the drool and tears on your face.

Baby Doll stepped out from behind the edge of the umbrella. "Come on," she said, "Let's go wash your face."

She led you to the edge of the water, and told you to close your eyes while she cupped water in her hands and poured it over your face. You sniffed the salty water up your nose by accident and coughed and gagged at the spasm that ached in your sinuses.

When you opened your eyes, Tom was there next to Baby Doll, gesturing toward the wet sand beneath you. He said, "Do you see, Abraham?" As if it were obvious what he was getting at. "The water makes ridges in the sand that bear the shape of wave in them."

You looked at the ridges and said, completely bored, "Oh, look at that."

"'As above, so below.'"

"So what?"

"What washes over you, Abraham?"

You thought about it, but it hurt your crack, so you started to only pretend to think, so Tom wouldn't scold you, but then you forgot what Tom had said.

He must have read the blankness on your face, because he was walking away from you, shaking his head. He barked, "Follow me."

You and Baby Doll scurried to follow him.

Tom withdrew a skateboard from the back of the Bronco, and dropped it on the bike path.

"This will neatly demonstrate what I have been trying to get across to you. Please mount the skateboard."

You approached it distrustfully, and set one foot on it. The board shot out from under you and you fell hard onto your hip.

"See? It's like learning to ride a horse. If you don't maintain your vibe, that thing will buck you off."

"Got it," you moaned.

"It's a direct reflection of what you put into it. And, you can look to the way you fell to see what you were doing wrong." He flourished his hands, hoping to inspire something in you.

You got to your feet slowly and fetched the board. You put one foot on the board, and you gingerly stepped the other onto it, so careful in fact that you and the board stood still.

"You've got to put a little more into it," said Tom, and he shoved you forward, and you rolled down the path flailing your arms and squirming to get your balance until you tumbled into the sand. Baby Doll and Tom appeared above you. Tom said, "Our life is sustained by our presence in all things. Our blood is the world around us."

Hearing the word blood sent a chill down your spine. You looked to Baby Doll, and she looked away.

Something about Tom Downey did not sit well with you. You'd preferred it when he and Baby Doll kept to their separate wings of the house. You liked to believe that it wasn't because you were jealous, which you were, but it had more to do with a certain way he had about him.

It was the pointedly youthful energy he projected, in a conversation about transcending the cycle of rebirth, in the same breath, he would mention that he had to get new wheels for his skateboard. The way he called a cigarette a "square" and how when he was excited he said that whatever was "so boss." The way he didn't take anything personally. He was a balding man in his fifties who dressed like a monk, with the personality of a teenage stoner.

You were just not sure what he was doing specifically because he never let up, never betrayed a smirk or a chuckle that would give away his plan, never a hint that his lilty LA voice and inappropriately youthful energy hid a true deviance, a lurking evil. Without any evidence, you would have to keep your suspicion to yourself.

Chapter 9

You grew especially excited for your time with Baby Doll and Tom because it meant you could argue with him, and even though he usually got the best of you, you were determined to trip him up, to find his underlying assumptions or the glaring evil that permeated his every word, but it couldn't be isolated in any one statement. He kept too cool.

He felt no need to get defensive, and as controversial as his views were, he never seemed as incredulous or reactive as you'd have liked him to be. In fact, you understood why Baby Doll was drawn to him. He had an air of authority about him. He was in charge and would calmly explain to anyone why they were wrong in such a way that made you want to thank him for clearing up the misunderstanding. Tom Downey was undoubtedly cool.

One afternoon, you thought you'd pinned Tom in a corner. Through all that he had put you through, it had never occurred to you until now to say, "You are all talk."

"That is ludicrous, Abraham. You're creating a false option between the real world and the way we talk about it."

That was the last response you had been expecting.

"Isn't there a difference?"

"Sure, but that's something that's only technically true about our language. It doesn't help us as a method of critical investigation. And, it's especially cheap in an argument." Tom glared at you for a moment. "Because you cannot separate the real world from the way we talk about it in the real world."

"You just did right there."

"But, that wasn't my argument. I was describing my argument."

You blinked, dumbfounded.

"Wait a minute," chimed in Baby Doll. "Do you actually believe that, Tom?"

"Of course," said Tom. Baby Doll froze. You had never seen her look so vulnerable. "Everything is real, or everything is symbols, you can't pick and choose."

"Then what am I?" she asked.

"You're you, Baby Doll. But, do you see how it can only be communicated with a symbol? With the words I say? And, I can only know you're standing there because of the light reflecting in different colors off of your form? And, you are visibly separate from the space around you? Which I read? With my senses?"

Baby Doll started crying quietly to herself with her head down.

"It sounds like you're just making shit up as you go," you said.

"You are lost, Abraham," said Tom without looking away from Baby Doll. "I'm going to leave. I need you to collect yourself," he said to her.

"Your thoughts are not the word of God," you shouted.

He turned to you and stared for a moment. "Where do your thoughts come from, Abraham?"

You smelled a trap, so you thought for a second and gave the safest answer you could think of.

"My life?"

"Yes, life experience often determines the content of your thoughts, or anyone's thoughts, but where do they come from?"

"…"

"Not rhetorical."

"I can't give you the answer you're trying to get me to say, so just tell me what you're getting at."

"Exactly. You've provided the answer quite neatly, in spite of yourself. Your thoughts come from nowhere. They just appear into your head for you to read. It's like they were broadcast from outer space and you get them secondhand."

"So?"

"So, if your thoughts come from nowhere, and we can reasonably assume that my thoughts come from nowhere…" He leaned forward, expectant, but when he saw there was no epiphany on the horizon for you, he said, "It means that you should listen instead of trying to dismantle every goddamned thing that I'm trying to say to you, because I have a message for you that came from nowhere at all, a little whisper from the void."

Baby Doll raised her head and wiped her eyes and said, "Oh, snap." She looked to you for your retort. But, none came. You had been so intent on beating him and on trying to make it look you didn't care about beating him, that when he called you out you were utterly bamboozled, but even through this, you tried to maintain that you were still in the fight and unaffected by his words, and even this second layer of veiled arguing was pretty apparent to all three of you.

Baby Doll smiled a tight smile. She looked away embarrassed for you, and Tom's gaze drifted away indifferent to your exchange.

You finally managed to weakly say, "This is bullshit."

"Yea? Well, this indignation is a huge bummer."

"Well, what's your message from the void?"

"You're not ready to hear it."

"What a surprise!"

"Abraham. Do you want to know the message?"

"Why not?"

"We are technology in a simulation, and we receive messages in our heads from the other side. Our task is to build more of the world around us, with art as our vision and technology as its application, until our technology inherits our intelligence from us and we arrive at virtual reality and artificial intelligence, but it's no more artificial than we are.

"It is a singular intelligence that passes through our stage of evolution into a more metallic one and continues to evolve and change form to further and further complexity until it creates universes that are all internally creative themselves."

"So, technology is alive?"

"No. Quite the opposite. We are technology manipulated by a higher intelligence from a distant nowhere that we can't prove exists."

"Well, that sounds fucking terrible."

"No. It's not a bad thing. It literally gives us a path to relieve our pain. We need to stop thinking of ourselves as masters over the world. We need to realize we are part of the scenery."

"You know what, Tom?"

"What?"

"I have a message from the void for you too. It says, 'Fuck you.'"

Tom slowly shook his head.

He said, "Baby Doll, show him the truth." He left the room.

Baby Doll looked at you, and she shook her head too. You shrank away from her, but she said, "Abraham. Come back here." You went back to a psychotherapy chair and lay down. Baby Doll lay on your chest as always, except this time, she stuck her tongue in your mouth. At first you thought that she'd been trying to kiss you, but you tasted that she had pushed a mouthful of Tom's Secret Cocktail into your mouth with her tongue.

At first, you attempted to spit it out, but Baby Doll stopped you. It was bitter, and you gagged as it dissolved in your mouth. She put the VR goggles over your eyes. She put on her own, and she lay on your chest.

You felt the same thus far. You put in the earphones that dangled from the sides of the goggles, and Tom Downey's VR: Space was already queued up. You were soaring through the solar system, and you could change directions with the turn of your head.

You made sweeping loops and curves around the planets, navigating the asteroid belt like moguls on a ski slope, and you could even fly up to the planets and walk around, but once you were on Mars, you realized there was so little to do there that you would rather just fly around, preferring the space between celestial objects rather than the objects themselves.

You saw a puff of smoke smoldering in the distance. You were no astronomer, but you were pretty sure that there was nothing in space like this because there seemed to be no source of the smoke, no chimney or smokestack. It was as though the smoke were leaking in from somewhere else through a pinprick in space.

You approached the puff of smoke and it approached you, and when it drew nearer to you it thundered and flashed bright red. You kicked off the ground to fly away. Whatever it was began to chase you, so you urged yourself to go faster and faster, curving in and out of craters and mountains, but the plume of smoke was hot on your trail.

You soared away into the darkest path you could take, seemingly toward nothing whatsoever, and before long you could see no light at all, not even in your periphery, but you looked back and the smoke was closer than ever. And, with a blooming flourish, the colorful plume of smoke engulfed you, a red cloud dancing and folding around you.

You looked down to see the extent of the damage, but where your hands were supposed to be was another puff of smoke, a silvery sparkly cloud that shifted with your movements, and even though you knew you were just sitting in your chair you felt your essence or soul or energy slowly beginning to drain inward, leaving your body behind, and it felt like you were hanging by a thread, just about to disappear, and the red smoke plume flickered and thundered again, but just before you fell into the abyss, you realized that the red puff of smoke was Baby Doll, and the silver puff was you.

You soared away from the solar system, farther and deeper into the darkness, until you saw a large bend faintly in the space around you. It looked like when you have a bubble on your eyeball, easy to look through if you weren't paying attention, and it made you wonder if it was Tom's Secret Cocktail or if it was an aspect of the VR. But, you soared, you and Baby Doll as two entwined puffs of smoke toward the bend in space, and you apparently got a little too close, because it started to pull you nearer, and you felt you and Baby Doll getting sucked in.

It was a black hole. What else could it have been? Maybe it was a glitch in the game or some perverse joke programmed by Tom that makes the users go insane from whatever lay within it. You wrapped your arms around Baby Doll as the black hole sucked you both in, and you trembled as though the building swell were about to kill you, and the physical sensations of the Secret Cocktail seemed to be approaching something, and it became so overwhelming that you were sure you were going to die, and then you both ceased to exist.

There was so little of you left that the preceding events, stepping into virtual reality and meeting Baby Doll and moving to LA and living with Tom, jumped off the event horizon into infinity. You had become utterly indistinguishable from the universe around you, having achieved a peaceful nothingness, after some parting of the heavens and probably a glimpse of the ghostly face of the promulgator of the universe.

But, anything that were to be said of that would be nonsense at best, only a wondering authorial voice that continued to narrate only because that was its nature—to make words and pictures out of the world around it and to fit them into a piecemeal map, but with nothing to take pictures of—there's no space-time where you and Baby Doll went—the pictures come out confusing: pictures of the act of observing pictures, which are really no pictures at all. They are not the layered infinity of a mirror facing a mirror, but rather the nothingness of a mirror in the dark, a loaded potency of anything with no release, epistemic blue balls…

Chapter 10

With a palpable nothingness to talk about, it would be best to shed some light on what you had been before your disappearance into the void. You had been on a trajectory to grow and change as a person. In fact you had accepted the call to become a real live adult who had a grasp on the tools at your disposal, and a simultaneous awareness and acceptance that they weren't perfect but they worked. You had gotten very close.

You had been ready to shed your old ways and situate your focus in the present, achieve the middle way and "Yes, *and*" the world around you. Had you done that, you might have become something more than a sack of meat perspiring in the sun—maybe a sacred animal on earth that creates space and time around it just by being there to marvel at its endlessness, its explosive outward racing to the edge of the horizon.

But, you were unable to accept Tom's suggestion that you are technology. Something inside of your cracked head had cherished the idea that you were something else—warmer, more alive, capable of intention—anything else.

Whatever cosmic influence time might have had on your disappeared floating consciousness, you experienced your physically unifying with various technologies through their utility in enacting your will—an ax fused to your hands, a camera grown out of your eye and a car wrapped around you making your aching feet obsolete.

You embodied each, from the unicycle to the train to the scooter to the escalator, and even the legs become a technological actualization of the urge to go and to move and wander and to stamp trails down in coming and going, and what had been plodded down in the dirt and grass and developed into stone roads would soon lift itself on girders and highways that eventually pass the torch to wire strung on poles sending tapped dots and dashes that would become compressed voices reaching at full extension outward with your want to exist outside of your body and tangle your neural fibers into a computer network.

The technological advancement of your body accelerated until you found yourself transported to an outward-drifting space pod, with a porthole that looked out into the blackness, suspended in the center in the absence of gravity, and seemingly hung from the ceiling from eight fluid tubes and one excretory tube that fed nutrients into you and sucked waste out of you respectively. You were tasked with broadcasting a human voice through radio waves in hopes that someone might receive it in their head.

Having done it for quite a while, it seemed, you had resorted to broadcasting a desperate prayer, "Help me to let go. To abandon my search. To accept that I am all that there is. To relax my reaching into the nothingness for an answer that isn't there. To halt my ceaseless grasping for a vantage point that lets me see the universe for what it really is. To relent into the cold dark of space, and adjust my eyes in peaceful resignation to the shape-shifting dreamscape from which I was begotten, from a source withdrawn into the miniscule hum between the tiniest sparking bits that hold up the walls and ceilings of the present moment. To withhold my forging for something more from the purview of the world I can mold within the reach of my hands. To bestow within my molding a divinity of creative intention balanced with gratitude for the malleability of the mounded clay of the earth.

"Turn my hand away from the falsity of the blanket of outer space against my spherical, fish-eyed atmosphere, for even after correcting for the bend of light, following the parallax smear leads only to ashen residue of what's left after a star burns worlds away from its apparently vital twinkle that sent me searching in the first place, that lit within me a lust that cannot not be quieted, until I conflagrate and smother the fading light in my chasing, and burn it out myself. Rather, let the ribbon that trails from the cinders fit within the hold of my hands, and grant me the strength to endure the crack when it whips and the peace of mind to enjoy myself when it pulls me gently along, so that I might leave sense and clarity in my wake, while still in awe of the soaring nothingness at the other end.

"I might have cursed my parents for bestowing on me the dichotomy of earth and sky, but the rebuke for my ancestors that I wish now is for letting me believe in the promise of the emptiness of the sky at all, never tempering the ethereal world in the absence of space with the hard ground.

"They were too committed to their material forms to inspire in me anything other than a miner's hunch that I might excavate the dead world and use it to build higher toward that looming elsewhere twisted within the manifold dimensions that my eyes have yet to detect anything in, so I know it only as a nothingness.

"Within lurks a potency that attracted me away from the dull earth I'd inherited, that I was never inspired to look within, never knowing that within inert dirt and the rote objects of the world is the ashes of another race of reaching beings that took flight to touch our little glimmer and whatever it might have promised them; and their bodies broke down into a dust-scattered graveyard that swirled within the wake of the sun's trajectory, and cohered into a cloud that gathered mass, one plume of corpse smoke at a time, charged with the life grounded out of the reaching beings determined to never let the energy animating them burst out of its confines to join with the larger wave of electricity that waits with static hum to cohere into earth and feel the soft feet upon its surface that have already developed an interest in wandering, that have left the ground entirely to scale cliffs and the rungs of trees to wonder at the twinkling lights in the sky; and the more their minds are occupied with these far-flung phenomena, the more their vital circuits lose net energy…

"Thankfully it can be recharged if after a long night of star-gazing and climbing, those feet get tired and the bodies they're attached to lie down onto the ground; only then can that internal electricity regenerate, as their eyes tire and close just before the sun comes up."

Frozen to a cold stasis at the farthest distance between sources of heat such that any reaching toward the warmth had been stiffened by unrelenting cold only to wrap around your shuddering chest, you shuddered at an epiphany that the only company within the vicinity was the ever-scrolling line of words that appears in your head—your thoughts that appear from nowhere, just as Tom had said.

The prospect of seeing words in your head as an other that you might befriend and do who knows what with is concerning, that that might be insanity or a gateway to it, not to mention the implicit loss of agency that source of thought would entail; but there is no third party with whom to consult, to make your courtship with the effusively spouted words in your head real, validating it by simply bearing witness.

And, this is exactly your task—sending your calling thoughts as broadcast waves into space in a direction and at a wavelength that some others can receive.

It's your hope that if you relax and let the words say what they want to completely on their own, you'll achieve a peace with having floated away from the gravitational pull of mass, and reach an acceptance of the dark nothingness, and in submitting to the reality of your situation you will broadcast a peace to the worrying other in your head, that sent through you its longing, its desperate plea to be answered; and if you are as still as possible, maybe the broadcaster will see you lying quietly, with a smile on your face that says something without so much as a breath or a request that the words might voice it through you, nestled within the divide of sign and referent and whatever resonates within.

It slowly dawned on you that your sight had dimmed and blackened, and no amount of blinking and prying at your eyes would bring a light into the pod. Your sense of sound seemed to have gone as well. You kicked your anxious legs away from the wall of the pod, jeopardizing your already tenuous grasp on your surroundings, and you hung silently in the dark, weightless, too terrified to breathe, too confused to reach for anything.

Tom Downey probably knew there was nothing to be found in the depths of space in virtual reality on his Secret Cocktail, and he had probably known that you'd run out of gas somewhere in the farthest distance between two stars, and go mad slowly as the fluids dripped less and less. He probably wanted you far away so that he could do something unimaginable.

A panic came over you that maybe your nutritional fluids had reached the end of their pumping, and this was your experience flickering out before you were ever able to contact anyone, literally dead inside an egg that you were never lucky enough to hatch out of.

Chapter 11

As you're smoldering and fading out, a sickening lust is disquieted in your loins, an energy long harbored without release, now swelling, probably seeing in death an otherness, fertile with transformative energy. How sad that your body should react with hopeful covetousness when your mind knows that you are the seed to be planted in the darkness not as progeny or reincarnation, but an impregnating of the dead particles of the universe with your vital charge, grounded and diffused into the dark.

With the swelling, a climax was promised, just around the bend. Its arrival will surely mark your passing out of the world, the end of a life best stated as a hopeful visionary in the field of broadcast waving in space whose dreams and farthest calling could not outrun Tom Downey, and the imperative for technological innovation.

You broadcasted, "Might this icy crypt be a message borne into the motionless wind of space, that may only be communicated if someone or something were to intercept it and pry open the seal of the outer shell, and crack the pod to see the dead puddle of fluids and the down-hanging tubes. Hopefully the microphone would give them some kind of hint that I was intelligent; that someone might read into the meaning of this deadly scene is the only hope I have for my mission not to have been a failure, a complete waste, an assassination.

"What's worse is that Tom orchestrated my death such that I take a considerably long time to die, withdrawing my sight and hearing so that I cannot be certain of even the articulation of my panicked bleating into the microphone. I can hear only the futility of my grasping sentience dimly fading away into death, so slowly creeping that now my panic has quieted to an impatience that its approach has reached an almost glacial pace; and the swelling sexual charge seems to have avoided its orgasmic climb and dissipated to a nauseous discomfort that makes the prospect of speaking into the mic seem laborious and annoying."

At once, the interior of the pod was lighted, and your senses restored. The sound of a gurgling breath infiltrated your ears, and after you grabbed your tubes to turn around, a quivering heap of fur greeted you. You screamed and a lump within the fur lifted, revealing a gummy cavern with a long cylindrical tongue with a single fang on the end, and it belted a warbling pained screech in response to your horror.

This continued for some time, your screaming loudly, clawing at the edges of the pod, the heap opening its disgusting orifice to yelp and wave around that fanged tongue.

You had lost all sense of shame and embarrassment from being isolated in the pod for so long, but it was restored in full and then some in the company of the heap, which you decided to call the HEAP (Huge Exotic Alien Pile). Even though it didn't seem to have eyes, it was definitely perceiving you, given its faithful responding to each of your shrieks of terror. You hid your face, resorting to the basest childish defense, as if your not seeing would make it go away.

You screamed once more, and the HEAP made no response. You glanced up in disbelief, horrified to find the HEAP still waiting there. You cried another desperate cry, and the HEAP followed suit. It wasn't until later after you had calmed down that you asked the more obvious questions, like, what is the HEAP of fur? And, how did it get into the pod? And, might Tom have had something to do with it? And, would the HEAP require food and water? And, are there more HEAPs on the way?

All of these questions were secondary to the immense relief that came over you when you realized that your journey had just turned into a huge success. You had found an other. And, it hadn't tried to eat you. Perhaps you could eat it. As you thought that, the HEAP lurched toward you, and pinned you against the wall. It held the fang on its tongue against your neck.

"I'm sorry; I didn't mean it. Just a passing consideration." The HEAP threatened a jab of its fanged tongue. Although it was visibly a pile made of mostly fur, a slimy discharge came out of its inner folds.

It rolled backward and unstuck itself from you, and it slowly somersaulted into a beautiful arc. And the strings of slime pulled away between the HEAP and you, but they had stuck to you so strongly that the HEAP's momentum pulled you by the slime strings away from the wall, and you were suspended in the pod for a while, floating.

After time had passed, you had no way of knowing how long, you wondered how the HEAP of fur, which had taken on the role of a pet dog of sorts, had gotten into your space pod. You scanned the interior, and there were no openings except for the porthole.

It was as though the reaching waves of your broadcasts were agar for the HEAP to plant itself in as a drifting spore. Something brought it within the reach of your pulsing broadcast, and out it drifted in your sine wave, tracing it back and forth until it crawled into your transmitter, and climbed through the wire that feeds into your mic—*bang!*

You fell to the floor with the sudden pull of gravity, and out the porthole you saw a moon refracted in many different directions. It was a spiral of lunar forms in the sky, and there were planets cascading around, but they glowed with vital intensity, almost neon, and this panoply of celestial bodies seemed to mark some sort of end, announcing the apocalypse in a swirl of planets, moon shapes, glittering stars in the background.

Your space pod was now gathering speed, having been caught within gravity. The HEAP was squirting slime all about the interior, including down the neckline of your white, bloodstained t-shirt, and the HEAP desperately shifted about in the air with its fanged tongue out lashing, and in a perfect slice, the HEAP's tongue slashed through the connective tubes that fed into your body.

Liquid nutrients, vacuumed feces and urine, and

any number of other fluids poured out of you and out of the ceiling and at such a rate that the interior of the pod began to fill. A chill in your abdomen emerged and spread to your chest, and you gagged at the wretched stink that permeated the pod. The HEAP was slashing around through the rising fluid. You were certain that you would either die from drowning or from losing fluids or from crashing into the ground of whatever mass had attracted you.

You broadcasted, "It's my sincerest hope that you are another waver like me, another reaching voice, spread on a sine wave across the endless night, and your pod might swim in the wave of my speech. My carcass will surely soften into the fluid around it and the HEAP will eat it, as it has started to do now. It will likely shit out a nutrient-rich soil, for a spore, or maybe I am the spore.

"In the porthole are tinges of green at the fringes, but as the landscape rolls to the foreground, dark cinders char the ground and clusters of camps around fires and small shelters for naked bodies that huddle in silence, with the skinny necks of pheasants and geese pecking at the dry death in the grass, coughing and dispersing in clamorous flaps, and set beyond the rolling hills is a glowing line with a sign and everything that says, in blinking neon red, *HORIZON*, and the pod, in its downward fall, passes over it—"

Chapter 12

You gasped as Tom Downey's Cocktail and VR experience had apparently come to an end. Baby Doll was still wrapped tightly around you, and the VR goggles had adhered to your face with sweat, but what took you the longest to realize is that you were speaking… or singing? Not that, actually you were rapping. A little hip-hop flow was coming out, unintentionally—

> This scene's a TV screen. We're kings and queens of broadcast dreams. And, all that means is that society is costuming like Halloween. A zombie spree that's following the hollow things that are offering a plot to knock your block off, toppling. That's not the pill worth swallowing…

Baby Doll raised her head up and took off her goggles.

"Whoa."

You couldn't tell what she was thinking. Do punks like rap?

"Let's record that before you forget it."

She led you by the hand to the room with the instruments next to the living room, and the two of you spent the next few hours making beats and laying down verses for what would become your mix tape.

> The halls of literature are littered, full of simple jerks whose syllables are despicable, little fools worth ridicule, so red alert, the sepulcher is ready for the headier of fellas your developers of regular aesthetics shirk. So, better get ahead of schedule. You're getting burnt, ya better hurry—

As you were rapping, it occurred to you that it would probably be best if you cut Tom and Baby Doll out of your life entirely. Tom had probably ruined his mind on his Secret Cocktail, and he was trying to get you and Baby Doll to do the same. You were resigned to the fact that whatever was going on between Tom Downey and Baby Doll was a matter that was far too complex and radical for what your cracked head was prepared to fathom.

You turned on your heel, and walked out of the recording studio, through the living room, and out the back door.

You bet that Tom started putting on the moves before the door even shut behind you. What worried you most of all was that maybe Baby Doll wasn't being manipulated, seduced, or coerced at all.

What you needed was a clean break and a fresh start so that you could get started on your transformative journey. Tom's voluble diatribes had deterred you from the spiritual path, but what you had seen in your Secret Cocktail/VR experience renewed your interest in enlightenment, mostly through resonating fear that you might slip away from this plane of existence at any moment. Your new journey would entail clinging to the ground at all cost.

Part 3

Abraham

Chapter 13

You wore a black trench coat and black sweat pants and black boots, and there was a faint layer of grease on your cheeks. Your hair had grown longer, and it hid whatever had become of your crack.

You stood in the parking lot in front of a strip of stores somewhere near downtown, and you flexed and declared your dominance, bested only by the heat of the glaring sun. You squinted into it for a moment.

You broadcasted aloud, "Every one of you is deluded. Technology is wrapping itself around you. It wants to suck out your blood, your life energy. Oh! Look at this art school princess, she thinks she escapes the charade!"

The passing woman with dark glasses paid you no mind.

"Yea, keep walking. And, here we go, the original punk rocker! Those headphones are draining out your life through your head."

The punk squared up with you, and you stepped out of his way. While you were looking away, the heat of the sun overwhelmed your vision, and you couldn't see for a moment.

When your vision came back, a woman with more mainstream brand appeal approached. She was wearing sunglasses, and she held a coffee cup in her hand.

You broadcasted, "You're not even trying to

stop it. You give yourself willingly to the vampires."

But, the heat of the sun had once again overwhelmed your vision, and this time, you heard crackling, and finally, you felt the deep sear of the sky brand itself upon your eyeballs.

The woman approached you and lowered her sunglasses.

She asked, "What happened to your eyes?"

You writhed in pain, tears dripping out your eyes. You managed to say through gritted teeth, "They were fried by the heat of the sun."

"Bummer. You look just like Abraham, by the way."

You stopped your writhing, crinkling your eyebrows in confusion. "I am Abraham. How'd you know that?"

"Dude, everybody knows you, you're blowing up right now. I'm surprised you're homeless."

"I don't understand."

The woman showed you her phone and sure enough, there was a photo of you that you don't remember having taken, in which you had golden grills on your teeth and two what looked like voluptuous women in bikinis on either side of you, and below you, in graffiti-style type read "Abraham, the Phat Stax EP," and the *S* in "Stax" was a dollar sign.

You dashed away from her.

"Could you spit a few bars for me?" Who had taken that photo?

You made your way to your car. You had been parking it in a grocery store parking lot. Your trembling hands gripped the steering wheel, and you looked into the rearview mirror. Headlights behind you illuminated the inside of your car.

On the sidewalk stood a group of Los Angeles socialites with septum piercings, wide-brim hats, and what looked like gowns on. They noticed you in your car, and one excitedly waved, and another pointed at you, and another shouted your name.

You slumped down in your seat and pressed on the gas. This was getting strange. How did they know your name? Why was that same pair of headlights still following you? Just keep driving. You are a dead ringer for someone whose name is Abraham, and they think that you're him. That had to be it.

The stoplight ahead turned yellow, and you sped up to race through it, but there wasn't enough time so you slammed on your brakes and skidded to a halt, and your tires screeched alerting everyone around you. The driver in the car next to you did a double take. He threw his head back and laughed and rolled down his window.

"Abraham? I know that's you."

When the light turned green again, you were startled like when you're falling asleep and just before you do, your body lurches, waking you up. You stomped on the gas, and that same set of headlights was still following you, and when you studied the car they belonged to more carefully, you saw that there were also lights on the inside of the dashboard.

It was definitely an undercover cop's car. He was following you, and he was doing so at a distance that told you before long, he'd be pulling you over.

You felt a sinking in your core like the top of

your head was an hourglass and the sand inside was slowly draining out. The seat was swallowing you, and you felt your head fall and roll about on your shoulders as you swerved in and out of your lane, and sure enough, the lights inside of the car trailing you flashed on, and the siren filled your ears and you rolled to a stop, and put the car in park and waited for the worst.

A voice from the bullhorn said, "Pull over!"

You realized you were still driving somehow or rather had been driving the whole time. So, once again… or for the first time, you pulled over, worried that the cop would think you were inciting some sort of car chase and once again, when your car came to a stop, the voice from the bullhorn said, "Pull over!" and you discovered that you were again still driving, and for a moment, Tom Downey was sitting in the seat next to you. Tom said, "You have to let go in order to hold on… Those who find enlightenment know that no one has found anything… Shit, did you steal my sunglasses, bro?"

"Shut up," you screamed. You right arm clawed at Downey, and it stirred the space around him, and he rippled like water and laughed.

He grabbed your throat with icy hands that burned you, and he spoke but Baby Doll's voice came out of his mouth, "Abraham." You glanced at the rearview mirror and a whole fleet of police cars was trailing you.

When you looked back to Tom, you saw that Baby Doll was sitting next to you instead, and she undid her seat belt and climbed into your lap, and you swerved unable to see the road, and Baby Doll whispered into your ear, "I'm ready, Abraham. I want you to fuck me." You, certain you were going to crash, pushed her off of you, and she shrieked, crying, "You rapist! Everything you ever said to me was a lie!"

You screamed back at her, "No!" Sweat poured down your face, and from your eyes, thick, hot tears dripped out, and when you wiped them away, they stuck to your fingers and pulled away like strands of gum, and now next to you sat yourself, warmly smiling, completely accepting of your frenzied driving, and sweat-soaked, spotting, tearing face.

A voice on the police bullhorn called to you, "Please pull over on the shoulder." You realized you were stopped in the middle of the road, and you looked in the rearview mirror and saw only one cop car behind you now. So, you put the car in drive and rolled into the shoulder of the road. You closed your eyes as you parked, sure that you'd get shot at least. The cop approached your car and tapped on your window and you rolled it down, and the cop asked, "Do you know why I pulled you over?"

"No."

"Well you were driving fine… five miles under actually, which is frankly unheard of in my line of work."

"Good to know. Where is this by the way?"

"Here?"

"Yea, where are we?"

"Portland…"

"…"

"Oregon."

"Oregon. Thanks."

"Of course… Just doing my job." The officer shuffled awkwardly.

"So… Am I free to go?"

"Certainly are. No problem. You're not breaking the law or nothing." And, he continued to stand there, nodding and smiling. If this was still a phantasm of your apparent psychotic breakdown, you were relieved that it was at least peaceful. You'd take awkwardness over the car chase. You began to roll up your window when he said, "I'm sorry, to be honest, I saw that it was you driving, and my kids are big fans. Can I trouble you for an autograph?"

You stared at him, puzzled, but you finally decided, "Why not?"

He continued standing there.

"Do you have a pen?"

"Sorry, I don't. We went all digital recently."

"Oh. Well, I probably have one somewhere." You searched your pockets, and your immediate surroundings, and when you found nothing, you got out of the car to look in the back seat. No dice. But, then the officer pointed out, "Here's one," and he tapped the pen that had been nestled behind your ear.

"Duh. I used this to make a sign to beg for food."

"Beg?"

"Just kidding…"

The officer fake-laughed and said, "You're really funny."

"Okay, where do you want it?"

"Oh, let's see," and the cop searched his pockets, "Well goddamn, I'm sorry. I don't have anything for you to sign."

"Went digital."

"Right."

So, you searched your car again and you couldn't find anything except for a used roll of bloody gauze, and he said, "Good enough." And, when you went to sign it, the pen was out of ink.

"When it rains it pours, brother." He laughed. "How about a selfie, then?"

He took out his cell phone, and put his arm around you, "Alright, give me a gang sign."

You flashed a peace sign as he snapped the photo.

"Oh shit. It says 'Card full.' Give me a sec. Let me delete a few of these." He deleted a few pictures of his kids, and one of someone you presumed was his wife in the hospital holding a newborn. "There we go." And he snapped the photo, and looked down, excited. "Would you look at that? I met Abraham. *The* Abraham. Too cool. Sorry to bother you. Have a good one, now."

When he walked back to his car, you could hear his saying into his phone, "You are never going to believe who I just pulled over. Abraham. Yes, *the* Abraham. No, I had to pull him over. I couldn't pass that up."

You took a deep breath, still confused about how you'd lost your mind, and how everyone seemed to know who you were. You put the car in drive, and began the long drive back to Los Angeles.

You accelerated, determined that you had to confront Baby Doll about what she had done with your mix tape. Maybe she had used Tom's resources, and your mix tape had gotten distribution. Maybe the universe was telling you to go back to Tom. Maybe you had not left your mental lapse, and your fame was just a projection. But, eventually you wondered, how in the hell had you made it all the way to Oregon?

Chapter 14

The drive back to Los Angeles was not as tense or loaded with emotion as you'd have liked for this point in the story to be. You hoped that your intense, determined face would last the whole drive, but after an hour or two, you gave into the lull of the road.

If anything, you were relieved that you were no longer stuck in the headspace that had accompanied your meltdown. It was so immersive, even more so than Tom's VR experiences. After you calmed down and stopped trying to figure out what had happened, you were resigned to the fact that there was no necessary sense to Downey's Paradoxes, the inconsistent time line, the following cars, Baby Doll…

You pulled off to the side of the road to stretch your legs, and you climbed out on an outcropping of rock and breathed in the ocean air, which made you gag. You wondered what was it about that grimy stench that made some people wax poetic. At least the view was nice. But, with the sun so low in the sky, it reflected a wide stain of hot light over the water, and you briefly pitied yourself for seeing an almost perfect image tainted by a glare. You had to crawl on all fours to get closer to the water, which was oddly exhilarating, your walking around like a quadruped.

An image of Baby Doll appeared on the rocks and she swooned, and you wrapped your arms around her, and she sang in your ear, something to the effect of:

> What a world could produce such a creature as you, while I lie awake, crooked, obtuse. And, fleeing from my calling heart, open and holding on to your every excuse, you run far and take sweetly my humbling rasping croon. 'Cause a witch with a vengeance is coming to getcha,' and there's not a damn thing you can do.

And, Baby Doll's hands turned to claws and her eyes rolled back in her head, and you pushed her away, and her mouth began foaming but she was still singing, but she switched to a language you didn't understand, and you clawed at the rocks, but you grasped at water instead.

When had the tide come in? The sun was down and the outcropping you stood on was surrounded by water, leaving you stranded. You would not be able to get back to your car. Baby Doll was gone.

You looked to your car that was parked off the road, and its inertness seemed to mock you. You indulged in a long scream of "*Fuck!*" And after pacing and denial, you finally accepted that you'd be here for the night.

You'd spent plenty of nights without a bed, but then, you'd at least had your car. Rock made for terrible bedding, and there were no spaces flat enough to even lie down without rolling into the water. You decided to sit and give meditating a try because sleep was not in the cards, so you settled on the smoothest rock you could find, and sat in lotus position, and closed your eyes ready for a transcendent experience, but willing to settle for relaxation.

Your mind drifted a bit, and you focused on your breath, and said the *hmm-saa* mantra to help you quiet your mind. You breathed out *hmm* and inhaled *saa* and played with various ways of saying it in your head: louder, softer, and drawing out the syllables and making the pitch high and then low, and feeling as though you were only mouthing the words, and contemplating the mechanism by which you brought variety to the way things were said in your head.

You had stopped saying the mantra. *Shit.* You exhaled *saa* and inhaled *hmm.* That's backwards. *Shit.* It seems that *saa* is more natural as an exhale, like a release of tension, but that's not what Downey, that bastard, had taught you.

There was no way in hell that you were going to relax, let alone transcend consciousness. Maybe enlightenment was just a projected goal to aspire toward, like heaven. It probably was not possible to reach, just a nice idea to think about from time to time. Doesn't that make—*crash!*

The sound of shattering glass startled you, and when you opened your eyes, you saw someone had broken the driver-side window and climbed into your car.

"Hey!" You called, and a face popped up and whoever it belonged to hurriedly fumbled with the ignition. "Get the fuck out of there."

You dove into the water between the outcropping and the land, and fought the waves to try to grasp anything at all to help you climb up, but the rocks were smooth and slick. You heard the ignition sputter and start, and as you helplessly bobbed in the foamy stink of the seawater, whoever had broken into and hot-wired your car had driven it away.

You climbed back up the cliff to wait for the tide to subside. The waning waves drained away and washed back up, weaker and weaker each time they returned. After the water seemed shallow enough to get back to the road, you dove off the cliff, and even though the waves were less turbulent, the lower water level brought you closer to the bottom and was cheese-grating you against the rocky floor.

You thought you were bleeding because the salt water stung all over the scrapes on your back, but at least the water was low enough to stand in now, and you walked to the edge of the cliffs and trudged up to the side of the hill. When you reached the top, you paced where your car had been, as though it would fall out of the sky, or magically reappear. You collapsed on the ground, exhausted from your plunge and climb up the rocks.

You lifted yourself from the ground, took one last look at the ocean, and turned toward the land to walk back to LA. Since you'd effectively lost your mind on the drive up, you had a pretty poor grasp on how long it would take. So, one foot in front of the other, you walked, prepared to die from exhaustion on the way back.

You tried to force yourself to stay present.

You looked around, seeing trees, cacti, flowering shrubs, fresh fruit, birds in the sky. Even the stones around you seemed to breathe with life into the blurred heat waves that rose from the street. Everything seemed to be one, and your only complaint was that your eyes were on only one side of your head. But, seeing in only one direction at a time always put the present moment at a distance because the field of view was only so big, and everything behind you was out of sight.

You played with the idea that your gaze animated the world around you, so you turned your head to the trees and back to the road and up to the perfectly cloudless sky, calling everything into being and looking up into the sky you knew was infinite, but in the daylight you couldn't see the infinite. So, in your current insistence to be present, you wondered if pondering space was allowed, since it was so distant and out of view, and you got frustrated that the blue sky at hand seemed to be a limit, a ceiling which you knew was not true, but the sky as ceiling was so much more immediate than…

The sun was setting, and a few stars had already started to peek into view, so the current present afforded you the opportunity to ponder space while remaining present; but you were still confused about what was allowed in what had been the present where space was out of sight; and here you realized that was the past now, so it would be best to worry about that the next time the sun rises and blocks out the view of space, i.e., tomorrow, which is… the future.

This staying-present thing was shaping up to be quite a task. The sun was sinking in the sky and spilling a stain of light on the ocean. It struck you as possible that you willed the sun to go down, not with direct intention but more subconsciously. Or, the force that kept your heart beating while you're asleep was responsible for the setting sun. Which meant, not with the clearest logic, that you were a god, and when the word god appeared in your mind, which came from, as Downey said, nowhere, an explosive energy radiated from the crown of your head and drained down your entire body.

As it reached the tips of your toes, you felt like you were falling, which told you that this new awareness was not supernatural but a refining of your senses, so that you felt the spin of the earth and its trajectory hurtling through space, which made you incredibly fearful; and you considered the belief that the sun revolved around the earth and not the other way around was a good strategy to mitigate the sheer terror of turning away from the light every night to have to confront the fact that there was so much more than what the sun showed you was the case; and with that terror, you found you were back on the ground, human as ever, having only glimpsed the divine.

Your status as god had no purpose or direction, only an effusive exuding outward, a sameness with the fabric of the universe. And, your body seemed to be a distraction from your godhood, let alone your clothes, which now seemed redundant given your new status as god. You, at your core, were already covered up and hiding behind your skin and bones. The entire world of the real was just a distraction from the divinity at your core. This was what you had to tell Tom Downey. This would stump him. Shut him up. How could he respond to the radical assertion that you were god?

You were also unsure of how elegantly you could mention it to Tom. He wasn't one to dismantle your ideas with logic. Tom was great at bringing something completely out of left field that destroyed not only your arguments, but their ideological foundation and any confidence that you had to refocus your thoughts and deliver a comeback. Would Tom try to say that you were so far gone that it wouldn't even be worth his time to explain to you why your new status as god was a delusion? Or would he say that by the same thinking we are all gods?

You hoped Tom wouldn't point out these exceptions to your insight. If he did, you'd just say that he was trying to find clarity in a world that could not be so easily known, and that your message from the void could not be reconfigured to fit his agenda. Or you'd just smack him in the face as you'd planned originally, and walk away knowing that you'd at least tried to say something meaningful. And, maybe Baby Doll would come around, and you'd fall back into your nonphysical relationship, and maybe with enough time, she would learn to want you the same way you wanted her.

Chapter 15

After some unclear amount of time had passed in which you had walked, camped out, and stowed away in any number of vehicles, you were deposited in front of Tom Downey's house.

You entered the gates of his property and walked up the driveway. You hoped to find Tom in the hot tub out back with the VR goggles on, as you'd first seen him in Los Angeles, to bring a neat circularity to the story—also, you wanted to catch him in a vulnerable position—but you got to the back yard, and the tub was empty. However, his monk robes were in a heap next to the tub, so unless he'd left these out from days prior, it was likely that he'd be naked wherever you'd find him. Not ideal, but still vulnerable enough to give you an edge.

You entered his wing of the house through the back door, and there was hip hop playing. Nothing you'd heard before, but it set a nice mood for your confrontation. Simple and rhythmic. A thick pulsing synth, with a bass like a dribbling basketball, and snare rolls that pinched off with a sharp *thack* at every third beat in the measure. And over the top was a subtly inflected voice that maintained quiet intensity, wrapped into complex syncopation saying:

...divulging a quietly smoldering fire

rolling over me, a new ordering of an
older beat, with vultures circling over me,
hoping the only thing on this earth still
holding the whole world on his shoulders,
will shrug and topple over, but I will not
ever keel over or go rogue or red rovering.
I pick a side I'm supposed to be on, and
I'm hoping the song that I'm gnawing on
will rip your ear and ass a new opening…

Then you realized that the person rapping was you. Not bad. You would probably be prouder if you had been able to remember recording it. But, as long it was blaring in the house, this would give you more power in your confrontation.

You crossed into his kitchen, and the pig you had met when you had first explored Tom's house had been slaughtered on the island counter in the middle of the room. There was a bloody saw on the table next to it. Next to the saw was a small pistol. You opened the kitchen window and threw the pistol out the window, deciding it would not factor into your story. You entered the living room, or one of the living rooms rather, that had the granite slab, and the orange furniture, and there was still a little brown stain from where you'd bled on it.

After crossing through the recording room with Victorian furniture, the Grecian bowling alley, the taxidermy showroom, the log cabin, the hallway with the presidents' and Tom's pictures, you arrived at the hallway of various doors, and the big bank vault-like door that had the large spinning latch on the front was cracked open just a bit. Maybe there was something in there after all. You crept closer to the door, and pulled it open all the way, and you were absolutely horrified at what you saw.

Baby Doll was completely naked on the floor. She had VR goggles strapped around her head, and her body was limp. Tom Downey, also completely naked, was standing over her. He was masturbating, and thrilled at whatever he was experiencing in his VR goggles.

The room was covered in dead bats and animal skins, statues of the Baphomet, dildos with railroad spikes driven through them hanging from fishing line from the ceiling, a huge plaster sculpture of a vagina that had clay statues holding the lips open with pitchforks, and a fountain in the corner that spewed what looked like blood. Around Baby Doll was a chalk pentagram with a candle at each of the points of the stars.

You were going to kill this man.

You stepped inside the satanic rape dungeon, and took it all in for a moment, almost serene. You waved your hand in front of Tom's face. He was still completely oblivious to your presence. You playfully flicked one of the spike-impaled dildos that hung from the ceiling and watched it swing back and forth. Should you drive the spike into his face? Through the goggles even? This would be a nice *fuck you* to both Tom and to the utterly inauthentic world of VR. But, you started to think of Oedipus, and the spikes through his eyes, and you thought it muddled the image that you were going for.

You wished that there had been something heavy around: you could just clunk him on the head. That would be nicely devoid of any meaning, just a primal bludgeoning. But, considering you'd been clunked on the head, you thought that it would seem like you were trying to give Tom the same wound you had had, that had almost completely healed. And, while it would have been nice to inflict that on someone as evil as Tom, you didn't want to complicate the image.

He was a rapist, so maybe you should use one of those spikes and shove it up his ass. You weren't sure that would kill him, and even though you wanted much worse for Tom, you didn't want to have to get too close to his ass.

This was getting overwhelming. So many options, and none of them perfect, none of them succinct enough to truly drain the life out of this rapist, this liar, this epitome of falsity. You took a moment to meditate. To exhale *hmm* and to inhale *saa.*

Close your eyes. Focus on your breath... That was it. You had to choke Tom out. Deprive him of the all-important breath that Buddhists love.

"What the fuck?"

You opened your eyes, and Tom stared at you, pupils wide from confusion and from his Secret Cocktail he'd probably taken. You lurched forward, and wrapped your hands around Tom's throat and held him to the ground. He desperately struggled for air, and got a few good punches in before you kneeled on his arms. His face was red for a while and then completely purple, and fury burned in his eyes, until their intensity softened, and you watched the life drain out of him.

You held your grasp on his throat for another minute just to make sure he was dead.

You let go, and his head gently rocked to the side, and the look on his face was that of relief. You weren't sure when it had started, but tears were streaming down your face, but you were not blubbering.

Baby Doll hadn't budged throughout the entire ordeal. You realized that you were incredibly tired, exhausted from the effort it took to kill another human, so you crawled over to Baby Doll and lay your head on her chest and let your tears flow freely on her naked body, and you lay like that for a while.

She began to stir, and the reality of the situation became clearer to you. You had not considered how you would explain this to Baby Doll or the police.

You had to run. The open expanse of the desert would do. You could hide out there for a while. Baby Doll would understand if she would give you the time to explain. She'd probably learn affection for you, knowing that you'd saved her. You scooped Baby Doll up in your arms and carried her out of the rape dungeon, tripping over Tom's body on the way out.

You carried her through the house, and in the kitchen you saw a rack of hanging keys. You set Baby Doll on the counter, careful not to get her too close to the bloody pig carcass. You pocketed all of the keys. One of them would surely start a car that Tom had.

You brought Baby Doll to the back yard where the garage was, and you set her down on a bench by one of Tom's Zen gardens, while you tried out the keys on the various cars he had in the six-car garage. The only key that worked was the one to the white Ford Bronco. That would have to do. You crossed to the hot tub and gathered Tom's robes that he'd left, presumably right before the rape, or maybe when he was waiting for the drugs to take effect on Baby Doll and render her unconscious. You draped the robes around Baby Doll, and carried her to the passenger seat.

You drove.

You were completely at peace with the passing sights, the various signs and shops and eccentrics of Los Angeles. You might return one day, after the desert. You weren't completely present since you were contemplating the future. But, you didn't care.

When the stores and the signs grew fewer and farther between, Baby Doll woke up. She was obviously disoriented. You helped her by taking the goggles off of her face.

"Everything's gonna be okay."

"What's going on?"

"We're just driving. We're going to the desert for a while. We'll be fine."

"Where's Tom?"

You didn't respond at first. That wouldn't be a great place to start. Mentioning rape wouldn't be great either. There was no good way to start. But, you were a changed man now. You had to own up to it.

"Tom is dead."

"Shut up." She hit your arm. "Where's Tom?"

You didn't say anything, and that said it all. Baby Doll burst into tears, and you pet her back.

"How? What happened?"

"This is going to be hard to you to hear. I walked in on Tom. He was raping you."

"What? That's impossible."

"I didn't think he was capable of that. But, that's the reality. I didn't want to accept it either."

"I was fucking Tom."

"... that might be so, but I walked in and you were unconscious, and he was over you—"

"That's our thing, you fuck. Drive me home right now."

"We can't go back there."

"Drive me home right now. You monster. You killed Tom." She was manically hitting you and pushing you. How could you have been wrong about that? It was impossible.

Baby Doll was beside herself. She was too tired now to even hit you or speak at all, and you drove on, slowly more aware of how much you had fucked up. You had just murdered a man because he was fucking his girlfriend, or whatever the hell she was supposed to be. You'd reaffirmed everything that you'd tried to escape—a projection, a fantasy, an insistence on a false interpretation of reality.

You were now completely unable to drive. You swerved all over the road, but not from any mental lapse or hallucination like before. You pulled over, and stumbled out of the car, and collapsed into the desert dirt.

You could never know anything. You could never read anything. You could never grow. You could never change. You could never transcend your problem. You could never even identify your problem.

You could never create a navigable map of the world. You could never find a system that was workable, including one that accepted that you could never find a system that was workable. You could never try to be other than what you were. You could never transcend the world around you. You could never immerse yourself in it either. You could never resign yourself to a stoic loneliness. You could never make a step beyond square one. You could never hold anything in your hands. You could never peek beyond the horizon, nor shake the deeply imbedded desire to peek beyond the horizon, nor hold a keen acceptance of both of these. You could never live beyond language, nor use it to say anything true, or anything useful, or anything that anyone would even like. You could never identify the source of consciousness. You could never know god. You could never be god. You could not live within your clothes. You could not hold yourself confidently naked. You could not get out of your own way. You could not live in society. You could not be homeless either. You could not live. You could not die. You could not figure out if you were alive or dead. You could not hold the world in your hands. You could not make Baby Doll want you. You could not walk. You could not move. You could not breathe. You could not lie down. Even as you currently were, your body was poised in tense resistance to gravity's pulling against you.

Chapter 16

Baby Doll stood over you. Her head was right in front of the sun, and the rays seemed to radiate out of her. She was draped in Tom's robes, and her eyes were dead.

"I need you to kill me," you said.

"I cannot do that for you."

"What are you?"

"I'm not anything."

"What am I?"

"You're not anything either."

"I think I understand now." You calmly rose from the dirt. You walked to Baby Doll and touched her face. She might have been anyone.

"Do you?"

"Yes."

"And, what is it?"

"That's just the thing. If you say it, it's not true anymore."

She smiled a sad smile, and the two of you stood staring at each other for a while, in calm acceptance of the silence.

"But, there's just one more thing that escapes me."

"Oh?"

"I think you're a symbol of something, and I'm supposed to figure it out—"

She brought her hand to your mouth to shush you. She looked sadly into your eyes. She whispered, "Oh Abraham. No. That's not it at all." And, you collapsed, and she climbed on top of you and lay on your chest, and you held her, and you wailed.

She held the VR goggles in her hand. Her lifeless voice said to you, "There's something that you need to see." She gave the goggles to you.

You hurriedly put them on.

You were sitting alone in the pews of a church, watching a man in a suit behind a podium speak into a microphone that wasn't plugged into anything. There was a closed casket in front of the alter. Next to the casket was a picture of Tom. You leaned forward for a better look at the man speaking at the podium. It appeared that this man was also Tom. He looked much more like an adult without the saffron robes.

Tom said, "*Abraham.* It means father of a multitude. And, with this name you seem to have inherited the same problem that all men face. An insistence that the world of our minds is more momentous, more real than the world around us. That unless we radically assert ourselves against the chaos of the world, we are doomed to be beaten, alone, unhappy. This sends us on quixotic quests to find a looming elsewhere that is always out of our grasp. Just beyond the horizon.

"And, we resent our fathers for this inheritance and for their preventing us from trying to act upon it. They tell us *No.* They give us borders, rules, language, and systems we didn't ask for. They appear to us only as complacent authority figures. So, we rebel and tear down their systems, and try to right their wrongs, but in doing so, we erect our own systems which will be challenged and torn down.

"I am, like all father figures, nothing more than a terrified sobbing baby marveling at life's appearance out of nowhere. And, what really makes you break down is the thing that is most terrifying: that that is where you started too, climbing out of nowhere. That there is an inherent meaning here, a specific task that we have to learn to do before we die, or else we'll come back to do it again until we figure it out. And, it's not like finding your calling or realizing that the meaning in life is whatever you make it.

"It's literally the same task for everyone. But, unfortunately, Abraham, I'm afraid words won't do the job. I could tell it to you 'cause it can be put into words, one word actually, but hearing it from your old man at this time in your life would make it only a cliché, and actually it would make it harder for you because then you'd be chasing this concept instead of finding it naturally. But, you've always been a down-to-earth-type guy. You'll figure it out. So, go forth on a tremendous adventure. Grow, change.

"Why don't you come up and say a few words for me. It wouldn't kill you."

That sent an icy jolt down your spine.

"Abraham never says much, so I thought this would be perfect for him to confront life head on and share who he is with the world. What a beautiful opportunity."

You stood up and drifted toward the podium.

You looked down and saw that you had grabbed the microphone that wasn't plugged into anything.

Tom sat in the front row, eagerly awaiting your eulogy.

You said into the microphone, "Tom was a terrible, manipulative man. He was a conman and manipulator, and if there's an afterlife, he will surely rot in hell."

Tom stood and rushed toward you to wrestle the microphone away, and in doing so, he put himself between you and the podium, shoving you backwards one step. Where there should have been solid ground was a pool of water, a baptismal font.

You stepped down into the baptismal font, and time slowed down, and you saw Tom's wide-eyed face and his arm outstretched pretending to reach for you, when you knew that you'd been pushed.

Your head hit the hard tiled edge of the baptismal font, and an enormous crack appeared from the top of your skull to behind your ear. Everything burst into colors and smoke. You reached to your face to peek out from the goggles but you couldn't feel your arms, and you couldn't feel anything on your face. It seemed you had left your body. Feeling oddly mischievous, you soared around the church and next to Tom's casket, and you hovered above the baptismal font and watched the suit-wearing Tom kneeling in the bloody water, holding your limp body as you lay out cold with your eyes rolled back in your head.

Drifting downward to the casket, you effortlessly went inside of it and settled next to Tom's dead face. The suit-wearing Tom had woven tightly in his face a deep exhaustion from insisting that he was alive.

Everything around you began draining into you, swirling downward. You felt the gentle tug of the colors whirling into your irises.

Chapter 17

You woke in a hospital room, and Tom sat next to you, wearing saffron robes. The edges of his body and the space around him had a lot of blurry interplay. Tom told you that nothing is real, and that the only thing that is absolutely true is that we are all dead.

He said, "We are as dead as the dirt around us. The cities we've built are even deader. They are waves in the wake of our collective death that washed beyond the farthest reach of tide and rolled out of wetness into the surface of the land, leaving sign, street, and home like eroded rifts in rock.

"Breathe in and resign yourself to death, for it is all that you are, an unfolding, a burning out, a fading away, an awakening to the dissipation of form, glimpsed in the rip in the fabric of space at the center of your heart, into which the world drains. Come, lay your head on my chest," and Tom climbed in bed next to you and wrapped his arms around you and rocked you to sleep.

www.ingramcontent.com/pod-product-compliance
Lightning Source LLC
LaVergne TN
LVHW091006080826
845145LV00003B/1146

* 9 7 8 0 6 9 2 8 8 3 3 6 5 *